Immortelles

Immortelles

Memoir of a Will-o'-the-Wisp

MIREILLE MAROKVIA

MACMURRAY & BECK
DENVER/ASPEN

Photographs in this volume are from the author's collection. Oil painting, "Mireille," by Artur Marokvia, 1935, reproduced with permission of Mireille Marokvia.

Copyright © 1996 by Mireille Marokvia
Published by:
MacMurray & Beck, Inc.
1649 Downing Street
Denver, Colorado 80218

Printed and bound in the United States of America

First Printing October 1996
10 9 8 7 6 5 4 3 2 1

Library of Congress Cataloging-in-Publication Data
Marokvia, Mireille, 1908–
    Immortelles : memoir of a will-o'-the-wisp / Mireille Marokvia.
        p.   cm.
    ISBN 1-878448-72-2 (hc)
    I. Title.
PS3563.A678I46   1996
813'.54—dc20   96-23011
                                                              CIP

        Immortelles interior designed by Pro Production.
        The text was set in Galliard by Pro Production.
        Project management by D&D Editorial Services.

Two chapters from *Immortelles* were first published in *Puerto del Sol.*
"Will-o'-the-Wisp in Vol. 30, No. 1 and "Sarajevo" in Vol. 29, No. 1.

My gratitude goes to Kevin McIlvoy
for his expertise and his generosity.

Because of John.

I don't believe in ghosts,
but I am afraid of them.

—*Mark Twain*

Contents

Prologue

I have not followed the path my French ancestors' steps traced for me. I have walked away with a German husband, I have lived most of my adult years in faraway lands, I have even adopted a foreign tongue to tell my story.

The ancestors' ghosts have followed me. I have, at times, caught myself worrying I might disappoint them. The most insistent, lately, has been my grandmother's. The grandmother on my father's side I hardly knew when I was a child.

She lived in an out-of-the-way village. We had no automobile then. She was too busy running the farmstore and café she and my grandfather had built. Moreover, according to my mother, I had become very ill every time I had eaten anything at her house, be it a piece of candy, a pickle, or a chicken wing.

It was from my father's stories that I knew about the diminutive, tireless grandmother who had directed scores of workers and servants, had raised orphaned boys after her three sons were grown, and had always been willing to help others find clear solutions to life's dark problems.

"The grandmother" (father's mother) and one of the orphans she raised.

When I was in college, I took it upon myself to visit my little-known grandparents. They had, by then, retired and were living in the house they had inherited from Aunt Rose. A five-hundred-year-old house that had thick cob walls covered with whitewashed stucco, a high thatched roof on which moss had begun to grow, and a red rose climber that held the front door in such a tight embrace, everybody used the kitchen door.

Close to the house were a small stable, a henhouse, a rabbit pen, and an enormous, drafty old barn. In a corner of the vast courtyard a giant lilac bush sheltered the outhouse. The yard's fences were rickety and the gates were rarely closed. But the garden, adjacent to the yard, was entirely surrounded by forbidding, prickly, never-trimmed hedgerows.

In the garden, pear, apple, and plum trees, their crooked trunks gray with lichen, were scattered among neat squares of herbs and vegetables, strawberries, and cantaloupes. Along the central gravel path were two wide borders of yellow, orange, and red immortelles. Only immortelles, destined to adorn every house in the family the whole winter long. In midsummer they were beginning to give out a faint bitter and clean scent that mixed oddly with the musty smell of invisible mushrooms. Only noises that made one smile broke the silence. The contented clucking of hens in a yard on the other side of the hedgerow, the proclamation of a rooster in the distance, the squabbling of cats over a cantaloupe. My grandmother's cats had a peculiar fondness for ripe cantaloupes.

The path led to a dark pond. Two weeping willows bent low over it. Glossy green frogs with golden eyes sat on their own pale green floats, hardly bothering to jump off when I approached.

Close by, a giant walnut tree hovered over Aunt Rose's little bread-baking house. The oven had not been used for years, but I knew the ancient, nurturing fragrance of baking bread was still there. Swept clean, cut wood piled up in a corner, the bit of lace curtain at the tiny window freshly laundered and ironed, the bread-baking house was a shrine. Pink hollyhocks stood guard on each side of the door.

Over it all lingered the golden glow of Aunt Rose's treasure.

On her deathbed, Aunt Rose had told my grandparents: "There is a treasure in this house. I have hidden it with my own hands. It would bring you no luck if I gave it to you now. One has to work for whatever one comes to possess."

My grandparents had searched for seven years before discovering bottles filled with gold coins bricked into the cellar's walls. All the children and grandchildren received three gold coins each. None of us ever knew how many bottles there were, bricked into Aunt Rose's cellar.

During my visit, my father's father paid little attention to me. I myself did not remember much about him. A prickly beard, maybe, and a mixed smell of snuff and eau-de-vie I had hated as a child. He had been a busy man, a farmer on weekdays, a hunter on Sundays, and a card player on rainy days. In his retirement, he worked in his garden from dawn to dusk and went to bed early.

One evening, my grandmother brought out the ancient leather-bound book in which the ancestors had recorded births, deaths, and important events occurring in the family. By the light of a kerosene lamp, we read together lines faded to a yellowish brown that she had read alone a thousand times. There was an entry she was very fond of: 23 March 1793, a time recorded in history as The Terror. In her great-grandfather's own hand was written the story of how, as an envoy of his village, he had walked in his sabots to Paris (some hundred kilometers) and had humbly begged the revolutionaries to release his beloved chatelaine from prison. "Your chatelaine!" men as fierce as beasts had said. "We are going to chop off her head, and if you don't go back this minute to your village, we are going to do the same to you."

My grandmother had great admiration for her ancestor's courage.

"And don't forget, he is your ancestor too," she told me.

On Sunday, she said she had a surprise for me. She harnessed the old horse to the buggy and we drove to the village where she had built and run the farm-store and café. It was now run by an uncle and his wife.

We pushed open the glass door and went in as if we were ordinary customers. One single long table was festively set. A dozen people stood around in the large room, all in their Sunday best and all my grandmother's age or older. Like her, the women wore dark, long, fitted dresses and white starched caps that concealed their hair. I was wearing a short, sleeveless, brightly colored dress, my belt fashionably low on my hips. My hair was bobbed. The old people proclaimed—I could not believe my ears—that I was an exact replica of my grandmother when she had been my age. Same height, they said, same hair, same eyes. Same freckles, they exulted. The men shook their heads in disbelief and delight. The women patted my cheeks, my waist, my buttocks. Their old eyes searching mine, they held my hands in theirs. My grandmother laughed her great, sonorous laugh.

It was eerie. The old ones had retrieved an image from their dead past, a trophy, I understood. I was the occasion for the celebration, yet I felt strangely unmoved and confused.

We were served, I am sure, a memorable meal I could never remember.

One does not trust eyes or memories that old at eighteen. My mother too had told me that I resembled my grandmother, but always with anger in her voice. I admired my father's mother, but I certainly hoped I would not have her hard life, nor come to the end of it in some dying village where there was neither a church, a school, a grocery store, nor a doctor.

Moreover, the whole affair, in an obscure way, made me feel unfaithful to the memory of my grandfather on my mother's side. I did not resemble him at all, alas. But we had held an endless dialogue, and we had shared an enchanted forest.

Eventually, with youthful callousness, I decided that I had inherited my grandmother's splendid health and my grandfather's fine mind. And, perhaps—perhaps also the adventurous nature of this dear grandfather's father who had, one early dawn, walked away from home.

My grandmother was a quasi-legendary figure in my father's stories. I saw her on rare occasions at family gatherings, as if from a distance. She had other grandchildren who were closer to her. I went to the university, taught, traveled, stayed in foreign countries as the fancy struck.

I paid her a short visit in 1938 to introduce the German artist I was about to marry. She cooked a hearty meal for the occasion.

A few days later I received one of her terse letters.

I have nothing against your young man, but, mark my words, we will be at war with his people in less than a year.

And we were. I spent the war years in Germany and for a long time my life was harder than my grandmother's had ever been. War or no war, her life seemed to go on according to her own rules.

When she turned eighty (my grandfather had died five years before), she summoned her three sons to her lawyer in town. She directed the procedure. Her sons themselves made three lots out of her possessions: three houses and numerous fields scattered over good wheat-growing land. The lots were duly recorded in the lawyer's formal handwriting on three squares of paper, which, carefully folded, were tossed into the lawyer's black hat. Each son drew his own lot.

"No squabbles on my grave!"

Two years later she was seen rushing through the streets of Chartres during a bombing alert. She could not be persuaded to get into a shelter. She had no time for that. Her old cousin was dying in a hospital, and who else would be there to receive her cousin's last words?

One night, at the time of the American landing on Normandy's beaches, two fliers who had been shot down knocked on her door. She never knew whether they were British or American but she knew what to do. She hid them, fed them, cared for them until they were ready to leave. She knew very well that if caught she would be shot.

When we were reunited after the war, I told her that, at the time she had been hiding those "boys," as she called them, I had been doing my best to help some "boys" go over the German-Swiss border.

She only shrugged. I suggested that it had been easier for me because I was young.

"In our family," my grandmother said, "we do what has to be done. And that has nothing to do with age."

When my husband and I decided to emigrate to the United States, we went to say good-bye to my grandmother. She was close to ninety. The neighbor who had always ironed her white starched caps having died, she was wearing an ugly black beret my sister had knitted for her.

"I don't understand why you have to tempt fate again and again," my grandmother said.

"Grandmother, we are tired. We are tired of the Germans, and we are tired of the French . . . "

"It's not the Germans. It's not the French. It's us. Don't you know that? It's just that we humans are not very good. And you went to school for so long! Got your head full of things that have no use and forgot plain old wisdom to live by."

Suddenly she laughed, a laugh that was only an echo of her great, sonorous laugh of old.

"It all goes back to Aunt Rose," she said. "Aunt Rose had a notion that your father was not meant to become a farmer. She paid for his studies; he became a teacher. And see what happened . . . "

She held my hands in hers, smiling and shaking her head.

Her face that had never known anything but soap and water was parched and old. And that black thing on her head was so sad.

"Don't wait too long to come back for a visit," she said.

I waited too long.

Seven years later, I wrote to announce my visit. I have kept her answer:

27 March 1956
You are coming in July, I understand. You will be too late. My sons and their wives have decreed that I cannot live alone in my house any longer, not even during the summer. They want me to go live with them the year around. One year here, one year there. Can you imagine? I am not going. I love all my children, I do. But, oh my God, one is so happy alone.

One month later, at the occasion of a mild cold that, she said, had spoiled her appetite, she stopped eating. She sat in her big red plush armchair and summoned the priest and the carpenter from her home village. She gave the priest detailed instructions for her funeral and told the carpenter to make her coffin slightly smaller because there was not enough space left in the family vault. Then she summoned her children and grandchildren. They all came except the granddaughter who had gone to America and had not understood her message.

She told her daughters-in-law where to find the clothes she had prepared. This included a last ironed white starched cap. She advised her sons on what to do with their inheritance. She spoke quietly, clearly, my father wrote, until the moment she turned away from the living to converse with the dead a few minutes before joining them.

In a few short years I will be the age she was when I last saw her. I am as short and small as she. And as frugal. But—her old cronies and my mother, each for their own reasons, must have seen whatever they wanted to see—my features are not hers. My nose is not the high-spirited nose that went so well with her laugh. I have the nose of my grandfather, the grandfather who smelled of snuff and eau-de-vie. If only I could laugh as well as she!

And yet, yes, at times, I could be my grandmother. Like the spring night I woke up with the certainty that doom had come to sit by my bed. First, I reasoned; I ate lightly last night, there is no reason for that iron foot weighing down on my chest. And my little poetry reading went very well. Really. I read better than I thought I could. The audience was perfect. No reason, absolutely no reason . . . I waited. Slowly, reluctantly, I had to accept that I was having chest pains. The chest pains that do not go away.

The kitchen clock struck two. I crawled out of bed, went to sit in the rocking chair by the bookshelf, and looked up "heart" in the *Merck Manual*. The pains seemed to ease when I was up, so I stayed up. I read the chapter on myocardial infarction, then the chapter on hiatus hernia. I smiled feebly at my dog. He had come to crouch at my feet, his eyes riveted on me. Oh, those dog's eyes. Suddenly he got up, gave my hands a thorough licking, and went back to his pad by my bed. A good omen. Still, I knew, this was very probably a heart attack I was having.

What does an old woman who lives alone do in such a case? This is America, remember. Dial 911? I imagined the commotion this would create and cringed. Call my friend next door? I knew I would not do it. I knew I would quietly wait for things to take their course as they were meant to. As if I were living in a tiny village that had neither a church, a school, a grocery store, nor a doctor.

The kitchen clock struck four. Without much thinking, I went to the kitchen, pulled up the step stool. The dog came back, kept close watch on me. I climbed onto the stool, got from the top cabinet a bottle of Old Grand-Dad a friend had given me years before, poured myself a stiff drink, swallowed it in one gulp. The pains vanished.

"Tomorrow, I'll call the doctor," I told my dog. "Tomorrow."

I am coming to the end of my long life, alone—oh but one is so happy alone—in my modest little house. No high thatched roof, no. And no cellar for a hidden treasure. But I had the house painted white, and I have planted a red rose climber in front. Red tempered by green against stark white, an image snatched from the dead past like a trophy. Last spring the climber bloomed extravagantly and sent up shoots in every direction. A good omen. I still have some remembering to do. My ghosts are demanding their shred of immortality.

Sarajevo

I believed him when he said, "Yes, I will marry you. Yes, of course, I'll wait for you." And why not: I believed what grown-ups said, I was five years old. Besides, this was our beloved family doctor speaking. If I had seen his eyes when he spoke, I would have guessed, perhaps—eyes do not lie as well as the mouth— but his eyes were hidden behind the thick lenses of his glasses. For all I know he could have been looking at my beautiful mother when he answered my feverish questions: "Will you marry me? Will you wait for me?"

My mother stood on the other side of my bed, facing the doctor. Her dark hair was gathered on top of her head like a crown. She was smiling. Her eyes were shining. Her whole face was flushed as if she had been the one who had a fever.

Our doctor was very young for a country doctor, and his light red hair made him look even younger, my parents said. They did not say, but I knew, that the gold in his hair matched the gold in my hair.

We did not live in the town where the doctor lived. Whenever we needed him—and we often did— my father would run down the hill to the grocery store by the church where there was a telephone.

My father was forever running. He held three jobs. He was the boys' schoolteacher, City Hall's secretary, and my mother's help. It was convenient that we lived in the compound that included the boys' school, the girls' school, City Hall, and the teachers' lodgings—the largest building around, after the medieval castle at the top of the hill and the church down in the village.

The minute my father returned from making the phone call to the doctor, a wait, at times a long one, began. My mother could not get anything done while waiting for the doctor. She walked from one window to the other, lifted the lace curtains, rearranged them, straightened the bedclothes, propped up my pillows, tugged at her dress, at her hair, and stared into the mirror above the dresser.

Eventually the doctor's automobile would come to a stop in front of the gate. If, by any chance, I had not heard it, I would guess from seeing my mother suddenly standing still in front of the bedroom door.

From then on I followed the events in imagination: The doctor climbing out of a quasi-mythical gray-green machine adorned with fierce fenders and bulging, eyelike headlights, the doctor peeling off leather gloves that were the color of his hair, pushing open the iron gate, stepping briskly across the yard, then up the seven white stone steps that led to the front door.

My father would have rushed to open the door after entrusting his class to the oldest pupil. I heard the sounds of my father's and the doctor's voices, then the sound of their steps as they climbed the wooden stairs that led up to the bedroom. A wave of happiness

The author in her mother's arms.

would wash over me. Another miraculous cure would have begun.

From the nearly endless first winters of my life there is little else to remember.

At last, the spring of my sixth year happened. Star-like flowers popped out of wilted winter grass, dead brown hedgerows turned snow-white with flowers. The sun and clouds played a game of hide-and-seek that I watched as if my life depended on who would win.

One Sunday afternoon I badgered my mother until she permitted me to take off my itchy wool stockings and the no less itchy wool garment that children subject to colds wore against the skin in those days. Then I went to sit on the stoop with Médor. Médor was a dog big enough to be ridden like a horse. He had white curly hair and infinite forbearance. We used him as a pillow, the cats and I. When nobody was looking, he shared with me the coarse dark bread that was baked especially for him. Médor was not permitted indoors, and so our friendship flourished only on warm days.

On that bright Sunday afternoon the yard was ours. It was a large yard serving as schoolyard—some forty boys played there at recess on weekdays—and as City Hall's courtyard. The firemen in red-trimmed blue uniforms gathered there every Sunday morning to play loud music on their brass instruments.

I did not trust the yard's ground of beaten earth studded with nasty stones. I did not understand why the wrought iron fence and gates were topped with unfriendly spikes. But the seven great horse chestnut trees growing in the yard were reassuring. And beyond the fence was a gravel road of a pleasant yellow, and people and animals passing by. My grandfather would come down that road riding his bicycle nearly every Sunday. And though my mother had said he was not coming that Sunday, we kept watch, Médor and I. We saw the mayor's carriage drawn by an old white horse go uphill to the castle as usual. And, as usual, a flock of sparrows together with the neighborhood chickens came to peck at horse manure.

Médor watched the chickens for a while, then stretched out, his eyes half-closed.

A roar in the distance brought him to his feet. The sound of a car horn sent him down the steps. Sparrows flew off, cackling chickens scattered in panic.

An automobile rolled down the road and came to a stop in front of our gate. A doctor's automobile. No one else I knew drove one.

I was not sick. Nobody was sick. I got to my feet in alarm.

The doctor—our doctor—got out of his gray-green automobile, walked around it, helped out a dowdy lady in a dress and hat of a too-bright blue. Then he helped another lady, slim, almost as tall as he was, who wore a smart pale gray suit.

Médor was at the gate, wagging his tail.

I jumped down the steps, crossed the yard at top speed, slipped into the garden, and ran, ran until the back fence stopped me. My heart was pounding.

After a while I heard my father calling me. I had expected it. I walked back. Slowly. I met my father halfway.

"Guess who came to visit us?" he said.

I said nothing.

He took my hand and led me to the dining room. The doctor and the ladies were there, sitting at the heavy round table. My mother was pouring Benedictine—her favorite—into tiny glasses—her best.

A celebration.

My father introduced the ladies. First the beautiful one, the doctor's fiancée, he said. She sat close to the doctor, who had his arm wrapped around the back of her chair.

"The doctor is going to marry this lady," my mother said, as if I had needed an explanation.

They were all beaming. And I was sinking into a hole, which I had done before, but only in a bad dream.

"And the other lady," my father said, "is the fiancée's sister. Go, shake hands with them."

I was too lost not to obey. I offered my limp little hand.

"And the doctor . . . "

I let the doctor squeeze my hand. I refused to look up at him.

This made them laugh.

They had tricked me. And now they were laughing. Anger, hatred, and shame choked me.

While they drank their Benedictine, I escaped, ran back to the garden. Médor followed me. Luckily.

Many years later, I tried to tell my mother what this had meant for me when I was a child. She was stunned.

The author, age five.

"The doctor had been joking," she said. "Didn't you know that?"

No I did not know.

"I lost all my trust in grown-ups that day," I said.

My mother shook her head in disbelief.

"Oh, how I hated them," I said. "I could have . . . "

"You were a strange child!"

I did not tell her about what took place in our garden that day. I did not tell her that first I threw myself on the ground, not caring about dirtying my Sunday dress, wanting to dirty it, most likely—a sinful deed to begin with in those days. Then, clutching at Médor's fur as if I had been about to drown, pummeling the ground with my feet, I wished they would die. And there, an image popped up into my mind, a gray-green automobile tumbling down into a ravine. The only ravine I knew, located at the entrance of the forest, right along the road that led to the town where the doctor and my grandparents lived. The ravine was overgrown with trees. Never mind—the doctor's automobile tumbled down to the bottom of it. I saw it.

I frantically described the scene to Médor. Médor licked my face. He licked my hair. He grabbed the collar of my dress in his big jaws and shook me as if I had been a rabbit. He let me go only when I calmed down and hugged him. We stayed together in the garden until the sun went down and my mother came to fetch me. She scolded me for being dirty and cold and for having my hair all untidy.

I did not care about the scolding. I did not care about anything.

A few quiet days passed. Then, one late afternoon, my grandfather jumped off his bicycle in front of the gate. I followed him into the kitchen. My mother was cooking dinner. My father joined us. Whenever my grandfather came so late in the day it was to bring news. Bad or good, news always reached him before it reached us in our remote little village.

"This is not good news," my grandfather said. "The doctor had an accident, an automobile accident."

My mother covered her face with her hands and sat down on the nearest chair.

"The doctor was not injured," my grandfather hurried to add, "but his fiancée has a broken arm, and her sister a broken nose." And it had all happened the Sunday they had visited us, in the late afternoon as they drove home.

"Imagine," my mother exclaimed, her face now flushed with excitement, "imagine, on the very day the doctor came to introduce his fiancée! What a coincidence! What a terrible coincidence . . . "

My grandfather grumbled something about coincidences. He always grumbled when my mother got excited.

"What is a coincidence?" I wanted to know.

"I cannot believe it," my father said. "The doctor is so careful."

Nobody was paying any attention to me. I went out and looked for Médor.

I was giddy. A little bit as if I had received some fabulous present.

Médor trotted towards me. Good, wholesome, dear Médor.

"They fell into the ravine," I told him.

He wagged his tail.

"A coincidence, a coincidence," I chanted.

This put us into a playful mood. We played hide-and-seek until night fell, my mother came looking for me, and I got another scolding.

I don't think I ever knew the exact circumstances of the accident. If I did, I preferred to remember my own version.

My father did not have to run down the hill to call the doctor any longer. I was well.

That spring was an unending feast. The garden was a heaven of bugs, snails, toads, and flowers where Médor and I were gods. For the month of May the horse chestnut trees lighted up with flower clusters shaped like candelabras.

Even rainy days without Médor's company were entertaining. I made them entertaining. I would persuade the cats to wear the dainty clothes my mother had made for my dolls, cleverly cutting holes into bonnets and panties to accommodate ears and tails. I would vaccinate the dolls' pink limbs or extract sick things out of their bellies. Once, a fight took place between my beautiful porcelain doll and my oversized, ugly rag doll. A porcelain face got smashed to pieces. On the hard floor, like something alive, lay the contraption that had made big glassy eyes and thick eyelashes jerk up and down. Fascinating.

On such occasions, my mother's anger and my father's dismay could be upsetting. But not so much and not for long.

In May, the mark on the kitchen wall that had told how short I was went up by one whole centimeter. In June, my grandfather brought another piece of news. The doctor, he announced, had married his fiancée's sister.

"She had been disfigured in the car accident, he felt it was his duty to marry her." My grandfather's face was a blank.

My mother let out a little cry. Then she said, "How noble of the doctor! How noble."

"Yes, yes indeed . . . " My father always agreed with my mother.

"Noble?" my grandfather said. "Noble?" His face turned purple. Here was a word that made my grandfather very angry.

I did not ask what it meant. After all, that the doctor had married his fiancée's sister instead of his fiancée was not that interesting. I don't even know whether I told Médor about it.

When, weeks later, my grandfather brought news again, I hardly listened. We were all in the yard under the great trees. Médor was asleep in the shade. It was a gorgeous day. A day for rejoicing. At my grandfather's first words my father ran to his classroom. He came back with a large map. He, my grandfather, and my mother pored over the map. They did not argue. They did not rejoice either, I could tell. There was one word I did not know that they often repeated: Sarajevo.*

---

*Sarajevo, Yugoslavia—where the assassination of the Austrian archduke, Francis Ferdinand, on June 28, 1914, precipitated World War I.

A lovely word. I sang it. I danced to it. "Sarajevo, Sarajevo!"

My mother had never screamed at me in my grandfather's presence. She did that day. She screamed something about a father and a mother having been killed.

"Stop dancing! Stop dancing!"

For days, all my parents did was read newspapers and look glum.

But then the Fourteenth of July was upon us, and everything bad was forgotten. The festivities started early in the morning when my father shot the cannon in the field behind the school—that was one of his duties as City Hall secretary. I watched from a distance. He stuffed a two-foot-long cast-iron pipe with powder and hay, set a match to it, and ran. There was a boom that everybody enjoyed except my mother and Médor. The operation was repeated three times.

The firemen-musicians gave a deafening concert in front of City Hall. On the plaza, boys up to their waists in potato sacks tried to outrun and outstumble each other for a prize. Blindfolded girls armed with giant scissors tried to snip dangling threads hung with trinkets. And at night a parade assembled at City Hall. The firemen-musicians led the way. Some twenty boys followed, carrying freshly cut young poplars hung with paper lanterns that had lighted candles inside them. I walked right behind the boys with my parents. The parade went down Main Street, picking up everyone able to walk. There were clusters of flags above doors, paper lanterns in the trees, and tiny blue-white-red luminous glasses lined the windowsills.

The parade disbanded in the field between the railroad station and the river. Fireworks fitfully illuminated the night, crackled, sizzled, misfired—mock battle sounds that made little girls shriek. Then, on the plaza, under flags, garlands, and lanterns, the grown-ups danced.

I caught sight of them, half asleep by then in my father's arms.

"Stop dancing," my mother had said. "Stop dancing."

Only two short weeks later, Médor and I sat on the stoop watching grown-ups play—my father and the village priest. An intriguing situation. My parents did not go to church, and consequently, my father and the priest were not supposed to be doing things together and be friends. But they were.

They were making, I had understood, a machine of sorts with which they intended to listen to people talking and playing music far away.

But grown-ups' games, like children's games, can be abruptly ended.

Suddenly there was a loud clatter. A man had thrown open the iron gates. He rushed towards my father, all the way across the yard, handed him a big roll of paper and a letter. Then he was gone, and the big green spool lay on the ground, the black shiny wire making crazy trembling coils above it. My father, climbing the steps three at a time, shooed us out of his way. The black robes of the priest flew behind him as he ran downhill. The church bells began to toll the way they did when a house burned down in the middle of the night. Bang! Bang! Bang!

I tiptoed into the house. My mother was starting a fire in the kitchen stove. She was crying. She stirred water and flour into a saucepan, cooked the mixture a short while, then poured it into an old can that had a piece of wire for a handle—my father's glue pot.

My father came in and embraced my mother. He said nothing. He picked up his glue pot and in no time was out into the street, the roll of paper tucked under his arm. I followed him. Médor followed me. We both knew we were not supposed to go beyond the gates.

First my father stopped close by, in front of the little house where the firemen kept their pump and their long canvas hose. The big wooden doors of the pumphouse were always plastered with pink, yellow, green posters that told everything people needed to know, from school schedules to festivities and programs.

My father pulled a poster out of the big roll and pasted it across the others. A sad yellow-grayish poster. Two little black flags crossing each other at the top, an oversized black title, smeary black print all the way down. An old man came. He read aloud, slowly: "MOBILISATION GÉNÉRALE."

"What does that mean?" he asked.

"War," my father said. "It means war."

The old man leaned a bit more over his stick, said nothing.

We went down into the village. My father pasted those ugly posters everywhere over the neat yellow, pink, green ones.

People came, women and old men mostly, since the young men and boys were still in the fields at that hour.

Some stared and said nothing. Some asked, "What does that mean, General Mobilization?"

"War," my father said. "It means war."

And every young woman and every old man looked as if my father had laid a heavy load on their shoulders.

Then my father saw me.

"Go home," he whispered almost. "Go home."

I obeyed. We obeyed.

The next day my father had an argument with the mayor. The mayor lived in the castle on the hill—a castle that had a moat, giant walls, four towers covered with ivy, but instead of a dungeon tower, a lovely white chateau. The mayor was rich. And old. He wore a dark green cape summer and winter.

"No, sir," the mayor was telling my father, "no, sir, General Mobilization does not mean war!"

"And I, sir, believe that General Mobilization means war!"

My young father looked as pale as the old mayor.

I did not know what war was. And yet, yes I knew. I had heard my grandparents discuss the war of 1870. I had heard my grandmother telling about the uhlans, the German cavalrymen, she had seen when she was my age—giant soldiers who roamed the countryside on horseback, brandishing long lances.

"Yes, yes. But the next war is going to be another kind of war," my grandfather had said.

I did not ask questions. Nobody would have told me the truth anyway. I kept watching. And listening.

One morning Médor refused to wake up. I found him lying on his side, stretched out, in front of his house. His eyes were not quite closed, but I could not make him open them completely. And he would not budge.

I ran to fetch my father.

"He could not take that beastly summer." That was all my father said.

He loaded Médor on a wheelbarrow, wheeled him to the garden's farthest corner where only weeds grew. He dug a deep hole, pushed the wheelbarrow alongside, and slowly tipped it. Médor slid off the wheelbarrow. Then my father shoveled all the dirt back.

"Go away," my father told me. "Go away."

I did not budge. I could not. Nor could I take my eyes off the dirt falling on Médor's white coat. I had to see it all. I had to know. I had to know I did not know what.

There were tears on my father's face as he buried his dog. I had never seen my father's tears before. They brought him closer to me. I had no tears. My heart hurt.

Then my father and I were holding hands.

"He loved the snow," my father said. "Do you remember how he played with the boys when it snowed?"

Yes, I remembered. I had often watched from the window.

"He could not take that beastly summer."

It made sense. It was reassuring even to know that one could go, just go, when one could not take something any longer.

In the same week the mother cat abandoned her newborn kittens. I took a dead kitten down from the hot attic every day for the next four days and buried them in the flower beds.

Then my mother became ill. Our doctor came, prescribed medication, and said good-bye. He was being sent to a city far away, where a doctor was needed, and he would have to stay there as long as the war lasted, he said.

My parents were upset, but I did not care.

By now all the men my father's age or younger had gone to war. My father had not because he had, he then learned, a lung ailment.

A long shadow had stretched across the most beautiful month of the year.

I was alone most of the time. My father was more busy than ever, my mother always sickly. Sometimes she would not say one word for days. I began to roam the village streets by myself. But the other children shunned me. Not only was I the teacher's daughter, I was the child who had kept her father while theirs had gone to war.

A new doctor was called to my mother's bedside. A black-bearded doctor who spoke little. His medications did not help her at all.

Once, my father had to go to the big city for one whole day. My mother became very ill.

"It surely is appendicitis," she said.

I ran down the hill to call the doctor as my father had done.

At the store, the grocer pushed a crate under the big wall phone and cranked up the machine for me.

I climbed onto the crate and described my mother's odd symptoms into a black mouthpiece.

"Go to the butcher," a faraway, crackling voice said. "Ask for a chunk of ice. Tell the butcher to chop the ice into small pieces. Put those pieces into a water bottle. And tell your mother to keep that icy bottle on her stomach until I come."

My father had returned from his trip by the time the doctor arrived. After examining my mother, I heard him say to my father: "I cannot find anything wrong with your wife. Will you please excuse me; I have sick patients waiting for me."

And so we knew the black-bearded doctor could not cure my mother.

My parents must have had long talks while I was asleep. I never guessed what was happening until the morning a trunk was brought down from the attic and my mother began to fill it up with our clothes—hers and mine.

"Where are we going?" I asked.

"To the nice town where our good doctor has gone to live," my mother said. "You remember the red-haired doctor . . . "

"And my father?"

"Your father is staying home, of course. He is needed at City Hall. You know that."

"I am staying here with him," I said.

My mother laughed.

"I am staying with my father."

"Don't be silly," my mother said. "A little girl goes with her mother wherever her mother goes."

"Why?"

Here was one of those rules that grown-ups made.

When my father came, he said, "A little girl cannot stay home with her father. She has to go with her mother."

"Is it like stuffed bears for boys, dolls for girls?" I asked.

My father smiled.

"Yes," he told me, "yes, something like that." Then he went on to explain that he would never have the time to take care of me, and that on the other hand, my mother might very well need my help on the trip.

I understood. I would have to go with my mother.

I was not the only one to be unhappy about our projected departure. My grandfather made a surprise visit one morning. He and my mother locked themselves up in the kitchen. I could not hear what they said. But when my grandfather left, his face was very red and my mother was sobbing.

Then my father's mother arrived one evening. This had never happened before. We had always gone to visit her and it had taken one whole day by train and horse buggy to get to the small village where she and my grandfather ran a farm-store and café.

It was odd to see her in our house. She was so unlike the grandmother I had known in her own big home with my grandfather, where her laughter had so often echoed in every room. She looked stern and awkward in her long black clothes. The only thing I recognized about her was her starched white cap. She had brought me a bag of candy. My mother took it away, saying it would make me sick.

I never knew what my grandmother and my parents talked about because I was put to bed early that day and she had already gone by the time I woke up the next morning. I could tell one thing. My mother was angry. She would not talk no matter what my father asked or said.

After a while she went back to her packing.

One early morning my father put us on the train. He stood on the platform under billows of smoke and waved as the puffing, hooting train hauled us away. We waved back, my mother and I, but by then my father had already been engulfed by the smoke. I started to cry. My face pressed against the sooty train window, I cried for my father. And for Médor.

My mother dried my tears, washed my face, hugged me, scolded me. A lady I did not know gave me candy I would not eat. The trip was long and dreary. We had to change trains. My mother was so afraid of missing the connection, we could not go looking for a bathroom. Eventually, I ran out of tears.

I could never remember anything about our arrival. I woke up the next morning in a room I did not know. A ray of sun was squeezing through the lace curtains and my mother was standing by my bed.

"Where are we?" I wanted to know.

"At the Providence Inn! And a beautiful inn it is!" My mother was pleased.

We put on our Sunday dresses and walked downstairs to a large, sunny dining room where we had breakfast.

I looked at all the well-polished wooden floors, tables, chairs, dressers. Only at the castle where we had

The author, her father, and her mother.

been invited one Christmas day had I seen so many pieces of shiny furniture at once.

Two slim little ladies came to ask whether we had slept well. They wore ample dresses made of a shiny gray-green fabric that rustled as they walked. These were the ladies who ran the Providence Inn, my mother said.

"If you need anything, all you have to do is ask," they told us. They smiled and rustled away to greet other people at another table.

After breakfast we went to see the town. This was the nicest town I had ever seen. There were rose gardens around every house, flowerpots at every window. There were shops and beautiful clothes on display. There were sidewalks, and the streets were paved. Grown-ups and children wore Sunday clothes. On narrow sidewalks, gentlemen would step down to let us pass and lift their hats. I could tell they saw how beautiful my mother was. My mother smiled. She held my hand tightly all the time. She was a different mother.

In the afternoon we went to the doctor's. We sat in a cool waiting room with other people. I was fidgeting. I did not want to see the doctor. Luckily, his wife came to greet us.

"Let me take care of your little girl while you consult with the doctor," she told my mother.

She took me to her well-trimmed garden, introduced me to her dog—small and shorthaired—and to her cat—a white Angora, the kind that does not put up with nonsense.

The doctor's wife looked a little like the maid who had opened the door for us. She wore a plain blue dress like the one she had worn the first time I had seen her. My mother wore frilly blouses, white, pink, yellow ones, and swinging skirts, and a wide belt adorned with a gold buckle always cinched her waist.

But the doctor's wife read stories, made lemonade, baked cookies. My mother never baked cookies. I was to spend many pleasant afternoons with the doctor's wife.

One day she had to write a letter and she left me with the maid in the kitchen. The maid was cooking dinner. "Come with me," she said. "I'll show you something funny."

She took me to the barnyard at the far end of the garden. In no time at all she had caught a duck and chopped off its head. Then she put the duck down on its feet. The headless duck ran down the sandy path, splattering the flowers with blood.

I ran screaming into the house. The doctor's wife came running. She scolded her maid, took me in her arms, and carried me to her bedroom. She washed my face, combed my hair, gave me candy, said silly things to make me laugh. And she assured me, again and again, that the duck had not suffered a bit. Then she said that, if we wanted to have duck for supper, that was what we had to do.

"I don't want duck for supper," I said.

The doctor's wife kissed me. "I wish I had a little girl just like you," she said.

"Why?" I was amazed.

My mother was feeling better. She spent hours with the ladies of the Providence Inn, helping them to make dresses for a wedding they were going to attend.

"Your mother is a wonderful dressmaker," they would tell me.

"Yes," my mother would say, "I cannot cook, I cannot clean house, but I surely love sewing." And she would laugh.

"If you opened a dress shop," one of the ladies once said, "you would get more work than you could handle."

My mother turned sad. "I live in a drab little village where nobody wears nice clothes," she said. "And besides, my husband being the teacher, I could not be a dressmaker."

Both ladies agreed, a teacher's wife could not be a dressmaker. No one explained why this was so, but that much I understood: Grown-ups too had to obey rules that make them unhappy.

I was getting used to our new life. I liked our walks through town and in the park. We also visited dress shops. My mother never tired of visiting dress shops.

We often stopped to talk with an old gentleman who sat every morning in his tiny rose garden, a big green parrot chained to its perch by his side, a gray striped cat seated at his feet. The parrot could talk. He and the cat were great friends, the old gentleman told us. The cat would chase away other cats or even big dogs whenever they came too close, he said. One day, the parrot greeted me, calling me by my name. For some reason I could never explain, this reminded me of Médor and I started to cry.

My mother told the surprised old gentleman that I was only a silly little girl and that she, my own mother, did not understand me most of the time.

One afternoon my mother did not take me along when she went to the doctor. The doctor's wife, she said, had gone to visit a sick relative and could not take care of me that day. She left me at a house close to the inn. There were two little girls there, Susanne and Lucie. I had played with them before. They were slightly older than I was.

That day a puppet theater had been installed in the entrance hall. A hall so large buggies were stored there in winter. The street end was closed up by giant dark-green wooden doors. The other end opened wide on the garden. On one side, one flight of stairs went up to the maids' rooms.

"We were rehearsing the Joan of Arc story," Susanne said.

I knew the story, of course. We were going to re-hearse the last episode when Joan is burned at the stake. The scaffold had already been built at the center of the stage.

"I'll do Joan of Arc and the bishop," Susanne said. "Lucie will do the executioner and you can do two German soldiers."

"German? The British burned Joan of Arc," I said.

"What do you know?" Susanne said. "The British are our friends. The Germans are our enemies. The Germans burnt Joan of Arc!"

I did not insist. I agreed to do German soldiers.

But before the play had started, the two girls began to argue about Joan's last words. Would she cry *"Mon Dieu!"* or *"Jesus!"* before she died?

Finally, Lucie said, "It does not matter, say what-ever you want. Jesus was—is—God, anyway."

"Jesus was not God," I said.

The two girls stared at me.

"Jesus was a man," I recited, "a good man, a man better than the others . . . "

"Who told you that?" Susanne asked.

"My father told me."

"Your father is a heretic," Susanne said.

"And you too," Lucie said.

The two girls took a few steps in my direction.

I began to retreat towards the stairs.

Joan of Arc, I remembered well, had been burned at the stake as a heretic, whatever a heretic was.

I began to climb the stairs backwards, keeping my eyes on the girls. I held onto the banister. Something was going to happen. Something had to happen. Anything. A maid would come down the stairs, maybe. But the maids were busy in the house at that hour. I knew that. The gardener would come through the hall to get a shovel, maybe. The gardener did not work during the hot hours of the day. I knew that too. I stared at the dark entrance doors, my last hope.

"My mother is coming!" I said. I was at least going to gain time. The girls knew that.

"Your mother won't come before four o'clock. She told my mother. I heard her," Susanne said. She laughed an ugly laugh.

"Heretic, heretic!" Lucie chanted.

Then the doorbell rang. So loudly we all jumped. It rang once, twice. A maid came from the garden, ran through the hall, opened the heavy street door. And there stood my beautiful mother in a rectangle of glorious light. She opened her arms. I ran to her. She bent over to lift me up and hug me.

We both shouted, "Good-bye!" and we were gone.

The heavy door slammed behind us with a great reassuring bang.

My mother was squeezing my hand so hard it hurt. I did not mind. She walked so fast I could hardly keep up with her. I did not mind that either.

When we entered the inn, one of the slim ladies handed her a letter. We got a letter from my father almost every day. But this one was not from my father. My mother looked at it for a good while, turned it over, shrugged. She began to tear open the envelope as we climbed up the sleek wooden stairs on our way to our bedroom.

I was climbing behind her. The steps were high for me. I held onto her skirt, the skirt I liked best, made of light blue-gray fabric so soft I wanted to rub my cheek against it. Her shoes of supple pale yellow leather were buttoned on one side. She needed a special hook to button up these shoes.

As we were reaching the landing, my mother's skirt roughly brushed against my face. At first I thought she was about to sit down on the stairs. I could not believe she would do such a thing. But no, she was falling. And next she was lying down at the top of the stairs, her head propped against the wall, her big hat all askew, her eyes closed, her hand clutching the crumpled letter.

Before I had time to call for help, the Providence ladies had rustled up the stairs. They held a vial under my mother's nose, undid her belt buckle. My mother opened her eyes. She looked very pale. But with the help of the ladies, she got to her feet. I picked up her hat. Soon she was in her bed, propped on white pillows, drinking bouillon.

The Providence ladies were quite pleased with my mother's swift recovery but they were going to call the doctor in any case, they said.

"No!" my mother screamed. "No doctor." And the color came back into her face.

The ladies looked startled but said nothing. They did not call the doctor.

That same evening my mother began to pack.

The Providence ladies put us on the train the next morning. They told my mother not to worry about anything. Yes, of course, they understood we had been called home quite unexpectedly. Yes they would transmit her message, and "Good-bye dear, good-bye."

They waved and we waved until we could no longer see them.

Then we sat in our compartment, the two of us. My mother did not talk. I knew she did not want to talk. Through the window we watched things drifting by, yellow fields, villages, church steeples, and telephone poles, telephone poles. It was hot. The windows were closed for fear cinders would get into my eyes.

The train stopped in some vast, dark railroad station. Our compartment filled up with soldiers. They threw their packs into the luggage net above our heads. They spoke loudly. They sat down, got up to rummage in their packs, sat down again. They smiled at us. They poured red wine into tin cups. They offered one cup to my mother. She turned it down, blushing deeply and holding me tightly against her.

The soldiers sang, drank, laughed. They gave me a biscuit that slowly crumbled in my sweaty hands.

Then, at another station, they got off the train.

"Good-bye, good-bye," they shouted.

"Good luck," my mother said. "On their way to the front," she whispered.

I did not know what the front was but I knew it had something to do with the war.

We had been so far from the war in the lovely southern town, I had forgotten all about it. I knew somehow that we were getting closer to it as we were going home.

My mother said I needed a nap. She made me lie down on the seat, now vacant, slipped a folded sweater under my head, and lowered the shades.

I was not sleepy at all. I closed my eyes to please her.

After a while I heard her open her purse, unfold paper, tear up paper. I opened my eyes. She was tearing up the letter that had caused her to faint. She opened the window. I sat up and saw bits of paper flying out, hovering over a field of high grass studded with tall white daisies.

My mother turned around, saw me watching her. She said nothing. She picked up the envelope that had fallen on the floor and put it into her purse.

The events of these days remained unexplained for many years.

One day that my mother was well—she was to drift in and out of depressions most of her long life—I told her about the day she had rescued me from two nasty girls who had been thinking of burning me at the stake as a heretic, I had been quite sure of that at the time.

My mother was not amused.

"Who was rescuing who, I wonder," she said.

Then, suddenly she told me what I wanted to know.

"That was the day the doctor declared his love for me," she said.

"Imagine, just when his poor wife had been called to her dying father's bedside!" My mother was still feeling the outrage.

"Ugly," she said, "ugly! Oh yes, yes, he said he would divorce, and I would divorce, and we would marry . . . "

"The poor devil," I said, "marrying his fiancée's sister because of her broken nose and then falling in love with a married—"

"How did you know?"

"I remembered. I heard you talk."

"Ah, children . . . And I always thought you were not paying attention to anything."

"I thought you loved the doctor." Now I was being too bold, maybe.

But my mother smiled like someone who has put everything behind.

"I was not Madame Bovary," she said. "I could not abandon the little I owned for a mirage. I got scared too, I guess. All I wanted to do then was to run, just run . . . to retrieve you, hold you in my arms, you silly, scrawny little thing, and go home. Go home."

We could not speak for a while.

"And the letter . . . " I finally said.

"The letter! I did not need that letter. An anonymous letter telling me that your father was having an affair with the young teacher!"

"Who wrote it? Did you ever find out?"

"We thought, your father thought, the baker's daughter, maybe. The handwriting, you know. I had kept the envelope."

I wondered why a plain country girl should write such a letter.

"Somebody wanted you to go home," I said. I stopped short. I could not tell my mother what I was imagining, seeing at that moment: my clever grandmother—her mother-in-law—writing that letter.

My mother wrote a novel during the first two years of the war. We knew about it, my father and I. We left her alone. The day she finished she burned the manuscript in the kitchen stove. This is how we exorcise our ghosts in my family. I never knew her version. She never knew mine.

Will-o'-the-Wisp

"Her eyelids would have jerked up like the eyelids of her china doll, I know it . . . " It was Léonie talking, shouting almost. I had nearly bumped into her when I entered the grocery store. She had been on her way out, her hand on the door handle. She paused to look down at me, then went on, " . . . if only those dumb farmers had lifted the long box at the head!"

I would have run away if my knees had not buckled under me. There I was now, wedged between the door and Léonie, clutching my coin purse in my cold, sweaty hands, trying to make myself even smaller than I was.

Léonie was a big girl and I was afraid of her. So were the grocer and his wife, who stood like wooden puppets behind their counter, well out of reach at the back of the store.

Léonie was a witch. I had known it the day I had seen her at the bottom of a pit full of serpents and toads, dressed in dirty men's clothes, high rubber boots reaching up to the top of her thighs. She had been laughing, grabbing serpents with her bare hands, thrusting them at a crowd of gawking villagers. I was very little then; my father had held me in his arms. There were only eels and fish in the pit, he had said. And they had come from a pond that was being drained. Léonie was selling them to the villagers.

My father was the boys' schoolteacher. He knew best. But he had not seen how the long coils of Léonie's golden hair had mixed with the green serpents like brothers, as I had.

Léonie turned her back on me and went on addressing the grocer and his wife.

"Oh, how I wanted to see her big blue eyes open and stare at the farmers . . . and at me in my ugly mourning outfit! She always stared, you remember? Forever wondering, she was. Wondering, never learning. She knew nothing of the world . . . would never have known anything if she had lived a hundred years . . . "

Léonie riveted the look of her green, knowing eyes on the grocer and threw back a strand of her golden hair over her shoulder. I pressed myself against the door so as not to touch the hair that dangled way down Léonie's back. Léonie always wore her hair unbraided, uncombed probably, tied with a piece of string. Nobody had hair like Léonie's, or eyes for that matter. Nobody spoke like her, either.

She rattled on, "My little sister was beautiful. Like a doll. Too much like a doll. Remember the dimples in her cheeks? Oh well, she is dead now. She died young. And, because she died young, she will be remembered like a holy image!" Léonie chuckled as if this had been a good joke. "Me," she went on, "I'll get very old and very ugly, and I'll scare people." She let out a cackle of a laugh.

The grocer's wife took hold of her husband's arm. The grocer's ruddy face got a shade darker.

Léonie went on, "Those three good-for-nothings with their red noses stinking of snuff, bottles sticking out of their pockets too, they did not raise the head of Solange's coffin as I wanted them to . . . They fitted the lid over the coffin and they banged on the nails shamelessly. You could hear the racket all over the house. I ran away, my hands over my ears, and I could still hear it . . . Well, so be it! . . . We will bury her tomorrow."

Léonie turned around abruptly and reached for the door handle. She stopped to pat me on the head.

"Where is your sling?" she asked. She did not wait for an answer. "Getting well, eh? That's the way it is . . . Some get well . . . others die." She ran out, slamming the door.

Our eyes followed Léonie through the glass door as she ran across the street, bent against the nasty November wind, her glorious hair flying behind her.

My sick arm began to ache. It was still aching the next day when my mother dressed me in the Sunday clothes and itchy wool stockings I hated. I knew better than to complain. In a few moments I would join the schoolgirls who were going to Solange's burial. I repeated the words to myself: "Solange's burial." They made no sense. Beautiful Solange with her sturdy legs, pink cheeks, blue eyes set off by dark eyelashes, her thick blond braids, so long that her schoolmates could dip the bushy tips into the inkstand of the desk behind her without attracting her attention . . . Solange could not have died. It was I with my skinny legs and red hair—to have red hair was not any good for one's health or character, people said—it was I with my freckled face and red-rimmed eyes who had been fated to die. At least this was, according to my own logic, what should have happened.

Solange and I had often seen each other when we went to the store with our mothers.

The differences between the two of us were stunning. But so were the similarities. We both had been born on the same day and month of the same year. We both had our left arms in slings. We rarely went to school because we were so often ill. I learned many years later that we had had rheumatic fever.

While our mothers talked in hushed tones way above our heads, Solange and I stared and sometimes smiled at one another. I had overheard a lot from our mothers' talks. I have never known whether Solange did. I knew what the doctors had said, that we both had a heart defect—whatever that was—and this was what made our left arms ache. The doctors had also said that our hearts would perhaps mend themselves before we reached the age of seven. Perhaps. But if our hearts did not mend themselves by then . . . Our mothers had never said what would happen. But I knew. I knew that one of us would die and that it would be me.

I remember how absolutely I believed in my own conclusions and how I waited in fear and excitement as our fateful seventh birthday approached.

It is not that I wanted to die—whatever that meant to me then. I did not. I even dreamed of escaping "my fate." Once, on one of my rare days in school,

I had seen a tiny mouse coming out from under the teacher's podium, peering at the class out of eager, shiny eyes, then vanishing. Could I, perhaps, survive as a tiny witness of what would go on in the world after I had died? So modest a wish could be granted, surely. This made a comforting daydream for some time.

Then events took an unexpected course. Two weeks or so before our seventh birthday, Solange's mother knocked on the kitchen door as my mother was cooking supper. My mother looked upset the moment she opened the door. She invited Solange's mother to come in and sent me out to play. I had never been sent out to play at nightfall. Something was wrong. Whenever our mothers had spoken together, it had been about us. About our health, mostly. Something had happened . . . to Solange. I knew it.

I ran all the way across the darkening yard, hid behind the gate, and waited, my eyes riveted on the kitchen door. The black tree skeletons reaching up for the cold sky confirmed my forebodings.

I waited for what seemed a very long time. At last the kitchen door opened. I heard my mother calling for me. Solange's mother was hurrying across the yard towards the gate. When she stepped over the threshold I seized her skirt.

"Solange . . . " I said.

Solange's mother was too worried to show surprise.

"Sick . . . very sick." She pulled away.

I followed her out.

"Give her a good rubbing with vinegar. My mother gave me one. Look, I am fine now," I said, my on-the-spot-invented remedy comforting me.

"Yes, yes, I'll do that. Thank you." Solange's mother started downhill, almost running.

The next morning Solange was dead.

I guessed it, I think, from seeing how my parents looked at me as they whispered together. If they told me anything I don't remember it. I asked no questions. I was the prey of my own thoughts. Terrible thoughts they were: Solange dying right after her mother had rubbed her with vinegar, as I had advised. Dying because of it. No doubt, because of it. Solange had died instead of me and it was my fault. "Some die, others get well . . . "

Long after I had understood that a rubbing with vinegar could never have harmed Solange, an obscure feeling of guilt remained with me. I don't quite know when I freed myself entirely.

No bells rang for Solange's burial—a civil burial. Solange's father, like mine, was a freethinker. Another kinship I had not been aware of until then.

My mother and I waited by the front gate until the long rows of schoolgirls came down from the girls' school. Only girls would go to a girl's funeral. My mother and the teacher, a young woman in black, exchanged greetings sadly. I entered the row at the very end, where a place had been reserved for me near another little girl my age. I knew her slightly. Her name was Odette. She had bright, laughing blue eyes. She took my hand and kept it in hers.

We moved in a procession down the street toward the old graveyard that surrounded the church at the center of the village. A neglected graveyard. Nettles and prickly bushes as tall as I grew undisturbed along a stone wall that was crumbling in many places.

We filed into the graveyard through the main entrance. The tall wrought iron gates thrown wide open for the occasion still showed traces of gilding on their forbidding spikes.

The teacher directed us towards the wall behind the church and made us stand in order. Solange would be buried behind the church since she was not baptized, and also at some distance from the other children's graves.

"When the Last Judgment comes and the dead rise, Solange will not be facing Christ like all the others," Odette whispered for my benefit.

The grave was very deep. I could not see the bottom of it from where I stood. But I could see the colors of the soil in which it had been dug, inappropriate, garish reds, ochers, and yellows in alternate layers.

Next to the grave the plain wooden coffin lay on a table covered with a white sheet. Close by, men in dark suits and women in black mourning veils stood silent in the sad winter light.

Four men stepped forward, put ropes around the coffin, and slowly lowered it down into the grave. A pale ray of sun squeezed between the clouds. This was when I saw that every man, woman, and child in the gathering held a tiny yellow strawflower—an immortelle—in their hands. Everyone except me. The mourners, starting with the grown-ups, walked one by one towards the grave and threw their immortelles into it. Incapable of guessing that my predicament was only due to an oversight, incapable even of turning to

Odette for help, I watched the proceedings with mounting terror.

Suddenly a black-veiled shape loomed at my side. A hand parted the veils, offering an immortelle. I seized it, looking up at my rescuer. Shimmering golden hair, green eyes . . . I stared at the immortelle in my hand. It was not a dream.

When my turn came, Odette had to give me a push. I began to walk towards the grave in a daze. Something was going to happen. What, I did not know, only that it would be the worst. Like being pulled down into the grave . . . I thought my legs would never carry me. But they did. I reached the fearsome pit. I even looked into it. I threw my yellow flower like everyone else. I saw it join the other flowers that were, by now, making a coverlet of pale gold for Solange's coffin. Deep, deep down. Far away. So far away already.

I returned to my place. Safe. I felt no pain. No pain at all. I felt nothing. Women wept loudly under their veils. Older girls had tears running down their faces. I saw them. I should weep too. I did not. I could not.

Odette took my hand, squeezed it a little, smiled. I smiled back, awkward, guilty, grateful.

Later, men shoveled the earth down into the grave. The sound of the earth falling bit by bit over Solange's coffin was too awful to be forgotten, ever. I wished that I dared to cover my ears with my hands. One could not do that, I knew. Nobody did.

Hardly a week had passed when Odette decided that we had to take flowers to Solange's grave, she and

I. We gathered the last chrysanthemums from the gardens devastated by the autumn rains. One late afternoon we slipped into the graveyard through the low wooden gate at the back of the church. It faced the priest's house and led directly to the area reserved for children's graves.

We asked one another whether it was proper to take flowers to the grave of someone who had not had a religious funeral. Neither of us knew, but we both agreed that, in any case, we should not be seen.

The children's graves were set in order along the old wall, small slabs of gray stone topped by faded wreaths over which angels spread their white wings. Baby angels, naked except for china sashes tied around their middles—blue for boys, pink for girls—were affixed to the wreaths by thin wires. The angels had the same delicate colors as Solange's cheeks, I thought.

"Solange won't get an angel on her grave," Odette said.

"Why not?"

"Because she has not become an angel like all the other children who died before their seventh birthday," Odette said, "and she should not, either."

"Why?"

"And you, you won't become an angel either if you die," Odette said.

With her merry eyes Odette could never look really serious, but her teasing, if this was teasing, had angered me.

"That's a lot of nonsense," I said loudly.

At that moment a noise coming from the priest's house right behind us startled us. We spun around and dropped to the ground at the foot of the stone wall. We had time to catch sight of the priest's mother, a tiny old lady in black. She stood at the open second floor window, her arms raised high. She reached for the two gray shutters on each side of the window to pull them shut.

"She looked like Christ on the cross," Odette whispered. She covered her mouth with both hands to smother a chuckle.

"She saw us," I whined.

Odette did not think the priest's mother could have seen us. She was so nearsighted she never recognized anybody on the street. But Odette thought it would be safer anyway to wait until it got dark. And so we remained crouched close to the wall.

My arm was aching. I knew I would end up complaining to my mother. She would then smear my arm with an ill-smelling ointment. Worse, I would have to wear the sling that made the other mothers pat me on the head with an expression of pity in their eyes while the kids would stare. At least Solange had been freed of all that.

"Let's go," Odette said. "She did not see us."

We were still holding our flowers in our hands. We had begun to quarrel as soon as we had arrived and had almost forgotten why we had come. At last, a bit sheepishly, we laid down our wilting flowers on the small mound of brightly colored soil that was Solange's grave.

We hurried back to the gate we had used to come in. It was now locked. We knew that the main gate was locked at sundown every day. We should have guessed that the two other gates would also be locked.

The low gate could be climbed over, but not at that hour. People were passing by on their way to the grocery store to fetch a last item missing from the dinner table. Through the gate's slats we could see, only two houses farther down the street, the big spot of light projected onto the pavement by the store's lamps.

Keeping close to the wall, we ran to the front gate. Maybe it could have been left open by mistake. It was locked.

Through the iron bars of the gate we watched people entering and leaving the bakery across the street. "It's dark already." "And it's cold too," they said. And "Good night." "Good night."

It would have been so easy to call for help! But that was a possibility we would not even discuss.

There was still another low gate at the north end of the graveyard. We reached it easily by walking along the wall. Across the dark street there was no one. But in front of the gate was a tall wooden cross. The bleak wood carving of Christ nailed to it was lit up by the bakery lamps.

I would not go near the cross. But Odette did. She soon ran back.

"Locked," she said.

We were not going to climb over that gate; we knew it. The cross was too intimidating even for Odette.

That left the wall. It was too high to climb. But there were low spots where it had crumbled, perhaps even a hole big enough for us to slip through.

We followed the narrow path between the wall and the graves. The tombstones and the vaults looked enormous in the darkness. It was hard to keep from looking at them. "Anything could be lurking behind them," Odette said.

She lowered her voice.

"When the Last Judgment comes," she said, "all those heavy slabs of granite and marble will lift up all by themselves and the people will sit up in their coffins . . . "

"Why?"

"Angels will take Christ down from the cross . . . They will put a shiny white robe on him. They will take away the crown of thorns and replace it with a halo of gold . . . "

"And . . . what is going to happen next?"

Odette would not tell.

"You don't know . . . Why don't you know?" I asked.

Odette had a maddening way of never answering my questions.

"Solange's grave is behind the church, she will never be able to see Christ," she said. "Oh well, never mind, she won't even wake up. And you, you won't wake up either."

"I don't care," I said, "I don't believe it."

The arguing was good. It kept us from getting scared.

Night had fallen completely. The moment we stopped arguing I began to tremble.

"I'm cold," I said.

"Quiet," Odette said.

And then she grabbed my sick arm, making me whimper.

"See it?" she whispered. "See it?"

And, of course, I saw it. I saw what one is supposed to see in a graveyard at night, the *feu follet*, the will-o'-the-wisp, the little blue light dancing among the graves, dying out, then rekindling itself a few feet farther, only to die out again. We had heard about the will-o'-the-wisp in all the tales that take place at night in graveyards. No matter what our religious beliefs were, we both knew that the will-o'-the-wisp was there to entice us into something terrible. It was worse than seeing a ghost.

We turned our backs on the graves and began to grope for a hole in the wall. We could not remember where we had seen one. We could not see much. Our hands got terribly sore. But we were lucky. Odette found a low place in the broken-down wall. She was strong, too. She dislodged a few big stones. We climbed out. Evil bushes tugged at our clothes, slimy stones tripped us. Nothing could stop us. Not even the fence of thorny bushes and nettles that, so far, had kept dogs out of the graveyard.

We could never remember how we made our escape, or what kind of story we invented for our parents' benefit to explain our torn clothes and why we had come home after dark. We never remembered whether we got a spanking or not.

But, even after many years had passed, whenever one of us would ask, "Do you remember the will-o'-the-wisp?" we remembered. And, long after all the tombstones, wreaths, and angels had been removed, together with the bones buried under them, long after my red hair had turned gray and I was the only one left to remember, I could still point out the very spots where we had seen the blue lights dancing, even though reason tells me there had been none, probably.

Shortly after our secret adventure in the graveyard, I came down with a fever and a cough. I was kept at home long after I had recovered. From time to time I would tuck a book or a slate under my arm, slip into my father's classroom, and make believe I was going to school like other children. I never stayed long. My parents let me have my way.

The doctor, the black-bearded doctor we were stuck with because there was no other around, had told my parents that I was a "nervous child" and that strict rules should not be imposed on me. A nervous child. I was a nervous child. Was that bad or good? My mother was a nervous woman, I had heard my grandfather tell my father.

This was the bleak first winter of the war.

Solange's tragedy, which had also been my tragedy, had ended. I was not sick. My arm was not even hurting so much any longer. The grown-ups' world was upset, busy, more remote than ever. I hardly ever saw my father. When he was not teaching school he was at City Hall, where unhappy people were forever demanding his help. I think I heard him laugh once during that winter.

He had just hoisted two flags on City Hall's roof— one of his duties as City Hall's secretary—the blue, white, red French flag and the Russian flag, bright yellow with a black eagle in the middle. A fascinating flag.

My father and the mayor stood in the school–City Hall yard, talking and looking up at the flags.

"The steamroller . . . the Russian steamroller! You are counting on the Russian steamroller?" my father suddenly asked. He laughed and shook his head.

The mayor turned away and walked out of the yard, knocking pebbles left and right with his cane. He was not laughing.

My mother did not have much time for me. She cooked the noonday meal for the schoolchildren in enormous pots that my father had to help her carry. Beans, lentils, noodles, potatoes, and meat soup once a week.

In the afternoon she put me to bed and locked herself in the kitchen—the only warm place in the whole house. She filled with her steady, clear handwriting the thin school copybooks that my father gave her. She wrote in purple ink, the school ink. I don't know how I knew, but I knew. My mother kept all the copybooks locked up in a drawer. I saw them only once, much later, when she burned them in the kitchen stove.

In the village, the only men left were old or sick and the women were forever rushing about. I saw them in the stores bringing little packages shaped like bricks and wrapped in sturdy white cloth. They weighed the packages on the store scales, then sewed them up all around the edges with strong thread. When they were not making packages, the women were knitting. My grandmother—I spent a few weeks with her that winter—knitted countless pairs of socks. I helped her unwind many skeins of rough gray wool.

She taught me how to knit. I started a scarf I could never remember finishing.

The packages, the socks, and my scarf were all for the soldiers at the front. The front, that unknown beyond the horizon, which darkened all life.

On the first of March, my parents decided I was well enough to be sent to the girls' school. Crowded, noisy, taught by a too-young teacher, it should hardly have been called a school. But I welcomed the change. I would have welcomed any change. I must have been quite well indeed at the time, and a bit light-headed too. One bright, crisp day, right after lunch, I got hold of my mother's big scissors. I was not supposed to even touch them. I hid them under my coat and ran down the street to the graveyard. I climbed over the wall at a well-remembered low place. I gave a furtive look at Solange's grave, a lonely little mound, still white with snow, tucked into the church's shadow, and hurried towards the other children's graves. They were free of snow. The angels merrily hovered over them in the noonday sun. I snipped off the wires that held the angels to the wreaths and shoved the angels into the pockets of my school smock and coat.

Back in school, I transferred the angels to my desk. At recess I gave one to Odette. Before the day was over all the schoolgirls, all the schoolboys, the teacher, and my parents knew. The village knew, the whole world knew.

An irate teacher and worried parents interrogated me.

"Why, why?"

I would not, I could not tell.

"Who told you to do that?"

"Nobody."

"What did you want to do with the angels?"

"Nothing."

"Did you want to put them on Solange's grave?"

"No."

"Why, why?"

" . . . don't know."

I often wondered. Had Odette dared me to do it? I would not tell then, and today I do not remember.

In the end my father gave me short pieces of wire and told me to return the angels to where they belonged.

I did as well as I could, hoping that an angel wearing a blue sash would not hover over a baby girl's grave, while an angel wearing a pink sash would hover over a baby boy's grave.

Afterwards, my parents and my teacher put their heads together and decided, with or without reason, that Odette "had a bad influence" on me. Consequently, I was forbidden to play or talk with my only friend. I would be kept at home for a while. Which was good in a way. I was, by then, deeply troubled by the way grown-ups and children looked at me.

It was the storm raging beyond the horizon that would save me from the village's reproachful eyes.

One morning our local train—three bright yellow wooden wagons and a locomotive of sooty black iron—brought its first gray load of war refugees. Drab women carrying bundles and babies, distraught old men, wide-eyed children, some clutching a toy.

They straggled uphill from the railroad station and filled up City Hall. We did not have enough chairs for them. They waited in silence for my father and the mayor to allot them a place to stay.

I, who had a father, a mother, and a roof over my head, offered candy to children who had seen a world just like mine crumbling. Children like me.

The village opened its doors to the refugees. Tales of horror came in with them.

My misdeed was forgotten.

There was still the interdiction imposed upon Odette and me, but the grown-ups were too preoccupied and too busy to enforce it. Children enjoy rare freedom in times of war. We soon turned the interdiction into a game of hide-and-seek. A forbidden pleasure at a time when pleasures were rare.

Odette and I met after school whenever I was sent on errands. Odette's house was located in the village, close to the stores. Her mother was alone now that Odette's father had gone to war. She did not pay much attention to us children. In her garden a big rabbits' hutch made the best secret meeting place.

On Sundays, when there were usually no parents or teacher around, we mixed on the street with other children. It was on a Sunday that we watched Léonie and her family moving out of their big house at the far end of the village. It was quite an event. People rarely moved then.

Léonie's parents had lived in our village only a few years. They had tried their hand at farming. Léonie's father had his own theories about farming. "Farmers work too hard," he had said. He demonstrated how to plant a potato field. No plowing beforehand. Make a hole by pushing an iron rod down into the soil, drop a potato into the hole, cover with dirt, and wait.

Léonie's parents had not done well.

The huge cart piled up with their furniture and drawn by horses drove slowly down Main Street. Léonie's mother sat in front, wedged between a dresser and a stove, holding the horses' reins. Her father walked behind the cart, keeping an eye on the huge load. Léonie led the horses by the bridle. Her golden hair showed at the back of her neck between her black scarf and the ugly man's coat she wore over her dress.

I was glad to see Léonie leave. Odette was upset.

"They have abandoned the grave," she said. "We will have to take care of it."

That upset me.

"I won't set foot in that graveyard ever again," I said.

"Why not?" Odette asked.

Forgetful Odette. She should have known.

Luckily, Solange's grave had been taken care of.

"It is like a miracle," Odette said the next time we sat together in the rabbits' hutch. "You have to see it to believe it . . . Thousands of tiny white daisies are blooming on Solange's grave. Makes you think Solange is still alive a little . . . "

"It is a miracle," I said.

"I always thought Léonie was a witch," I said.

Odette laughed.

"Léonie is not a witch," she said. "Don't you know . . . a witch is always old."

No, I had not known. I was glad in a way.

"But then how come she is ugly and beautiful at the same time? Nasty and good at the same time?"

Odette was laughing again.

"Léonie is just weird," she said. "Older girls are weird . . . They are like grown-ups, you can't understand them."

This did not worry her. Odette never worried over life's mysteries.

She had stopped urging me to go see the flowers on Solange's grave. She often went, she said. Even at nightfall. Once she had seen a little white form hovering over the grave, then fluttering away into the summer night. I did not know whether to believe her or not. I did not tell her. We did not quarrel any longer.

I never went to see the flowers on Solange's grave. Nevertheless, they are engraved in my memory, thousands of them, always in bloom, always fresh and cool in the shadow of the church—even though, perhaps, they existed only in Odette's imagination.

The summer vacation was upon us. There were no end-of-school ceremonies and no Fourteenth of July celebrations.

It was at about that time that the sparkle went out of Odette's eyes. Her father had been killed at the front.

I remembered Odette's father. He had had her same merry eyes.

I could not meet Odette for some time. One evening when I had gone to the bakery with my mother, I saw her passing by. I left my mother's side to join Odette. My mother did not call me back.

I took Odette's hand. We walked together on the darkening street.

"My father was a good father," Odette said. "He went to paradise."

"Yes, Odette, yes, he did."

I ran back to my mother. She had waited for me. She said nothing.

Shortly after, my parents decided that I needed a "change of air." I would go to stay for a while with my grandparents who lived in the town beyond the forest.

My grandfather came to fetch me. We took the gravel road that crossed the forest. He rode his big bicycle, I rode my small bicycle. We had to walk part of the way because the road went up and down quite steeply at times and I was neither a skilled nor a strong bicycle rider. The dark forest looming closely intimidated and intrigued me. I could hardly keep my eyes on the road.

My grandfather and I were to ride or walk through the forest very often. My grandfather gathered wood for the winter. Often, we walked along shady, hidden paths where nobody ever walked, or so it seemed.

Once, I began to tell my grandfather about an enchanted forest out of a fairy tale.

"This is an enchanted forest," my grandfather said.

And this was the truth.

There were the shy animals, so close to us at times, we could have touched them had we known they were there. We walked among them as if blind and deaf, while they watched our every move, anticipated our steps, guessed our intentions. Catching sight of one of them—a deer, fox, rabbit, blue jay, or salamander—

"The grandfather" (mother's father).

was a priceless reward. I tried to be as quiet, as watch-
ful, as wise as they. I never fooled them.

And there were the plants. The moss, soft and
deep, carpeted the forest floor like fur. I pulled up a
clump once. Its magic green died on the way home. I
could never revive it. Stems of foxglove shot out of the

luminous moss. They were nearly as tall as I was. They were hung with bell-shaped pink flowers bigger than my biggest finger. Surely there was honey in them!

"Poisonous," my grandfather said.

Not to the furry bumblebees that crawled into them and came out yellow with pollen.

Poisonous, miraculous foxglove. From its dried leaves a medication was made that kept my grandmother's heart beating, my grandfather said. My grandmother, who always knew when bad dreams invaded my sleep, who always guessed which food I would eat, who never betrayed my secrets . . . I owed my grandmother's life to a wondrous plant of the forest!

Then there were the tall ferns spreading the umbrellas of their lacelike leaves above the foxglove. We gathered these fine leaves, dried them in the attic, and with them stuffed pillows and mattresses that remained fragrant and healthful for one whole year.

Way above the ferns, flowers, and moss, tall trees extended a green canopy where the sun cut out stars of all sizes and birds without number sang and raised their families.

My grandfather said that the trees had already been tall and big when his great-grandfather had been a little boy and that they would still be there when my great-grandchildren would have children.

"A forest," my grandfather said, "lives forever."

My grandfather was wrong. Twenty short years after his death, our enchanted forest would be completely razed during another war.

My grandmother and I did not go to the forest. We went to the fields to gather wheat, oats, and barley

The author's mother bicycling through the forest.

left on the ground after the harvest. We would gather enough to feed our chickens for the winter. From the fields up on the plateau north of town we could hear the thunder the monstrous guns made.

My grandmother told me once more how, when she had been a little girl my age, the uhlans had banged on the door of her parents' farm in the middle of the night. They had made her father load up a cart with the hay he badly needed for his own cows. They had made her mother light a fire in the fireplace and serve them cider. When they left, one of the uhlans had pressed coins into her hand.

As soon as the uhlans had gone, my grandmother's mother had made her little girl throw the coins into the fire and had scrubbed her hand until it hurt.

The fear of long ago was still with us as we listened to the ominous thunder.

One evening, I told my grandfather about the rumblings of the big guns I had heard.

"They are stuck," he said.

He showed me the map that was printed big on the first page of his newspaper.

"Here is Paris," he said. He pointed to a big round dot in the middle of the map. With his finger he followed a thick black line that dipped low towards Paris.

"This is where they were one year ago," he said.

He followed a dotted line drawn beyond the thick one.

"This is where they are now. They are stuck there . . . We are all stuck there."

My grandfather looked at the map for a long time.

"This war is not going to be like the war of 1870,"

he said. "In 1870 they camped in the middle of our town. We called them Prussians then. I was fourteen. I was insolent. I would go to them and ask for food. 'You are eating our food,' I would tell them. 'Give me some of our food, I am hungry.'"

"Did they?"

"They gave me bread. But in the end, they kicked me out. And they wore nasty boots, too . . . "

"Why?"

"I had told them something they did not like . . . "

"What? What did you tell them?"

No matter how much I begged, my grandfather never told me what he had said to the Prussians, back in 1870, when he was a boy of fourteen.

I returned home in September. I had grown a little and I had learned to eat. My parents decided that I would enter school on the first of October like the other children.

There was still one long month to go until then.

The village children did not come my way. I was not sent down to the village any longer.

For some reason, the old games like putting dolls' clothes on the cats and wheeling them around in my dolls' carriage had lost their appeal. The cats were busy outdoors anyway.

I often sat alone on the stoop in the front yard. The horse chestnut trees were still thick and green. The prickly hulls of their shiny brown fruit were splitting. They were hard as stones and bitter. Even the hungriest animals would not touch them. Odette and I had gathered them the past fall and we had made gigantic necklaces out of them.

On the road beyond the iron fence, villagers passed by on their way to the fields mornings and evenings. The children who went with them were older. They did not even look my way.

The garden was just right for playing. It had sandy paths that went around beds of vegetables and flowers and many old gnarled pear trees that were easy to climb.

In the center of the garden was a summer house covered with honeysuckle and tiny purple roses.

A small toad had established himself in one corner of the summer house. I watched him crawl out of his underground lodgings and hop to the sorrel patch one late afternoon. In the morning I saw him returning home.

I decided to settle in the opposite corner of the summer house. I brought in my toy stove, bed, table, and chairs. I got busy arranging and rearranging them as one does when expecting visitors. Nobody came. The summer house was cold in September. I soon abandoned it to the self-sufficient toad.

The shortening last days of summer stretched endlessly. I often waited for Odette, knowing all the while that she would not come. I watched the two low wooden gates of the garden. One led to the front yard, the other to the fields in back of the schoolhouse. At times I would make believe that someone was at one of the gates waving. I would go to the gate, open it, greet and welcome my imaginary visitor, only to feel more lonely later.

One evening, when the sun had just gone down in a big red sky, a little girl my age showed up at the back gate. I first noticed her eyes. They were of a very pale blue, looking towards me but not at me. This kept me from rushing to her. Her elbows were propped up on top of the gate, her chin rested on her hands. Through the gate's slats I could see her long, loose, sun-bleached hair and her dress of a washed-away blue.

I knew this girl. I waited for her to say something. She did not. I finally walked towards her. By the time I reached the gate she was gone.

I opened the gate and stepped out. The girl was nowhere to be seen. There were a few houses toward the south but they were far away. She could never have reached them in the short time it had taken me to walk to the gate. In front of me the fields stretched far out to the horizon, empty at this late hour.

The only place where she could have been hiding was the high, untidy hedgerow that separated our garden from the fields. But why should she hide? I did not search for her, perhaps because it was suppertime and I could hear my mother calling.

The following day, at dusk, I waited for the girl to show up at the back gate. She did not. But later, I saw her walking through the fields in the distance. With her discolored blue dress and her long, pale blond hair falling loose down her back, she looked more like a girl out of a fairy tale than a village girl.

Soon I was waiting for her the whole day long, wherever I happened to be.

One afternoon I was sitting on the stoop in the front yard. I suddenly thought that she was sitting near me. I looked. She was. I had not heard her coming.

Her name was Madeleine. Whether she told me or whether I guessed, I could never remember. Anyway, this is what I called her, Madeleine.

She did not say much besides "hello" and "good night." Because I had so much to tell her, probably.

She came often. We sat on the stoop. We walked in the garden. We did not play. Butterflies liked to sit on her long blond hair.

I told her about my parents, Odette, the big guns, my grandfather, the enchanted forest. But mostly I told her about Médor. Médor could tell the time better than my father's watch, I said. At recess time, exactly, he would stand on his hind legs and look through the glass top of the schoolroom door. The boys would jump up and my father would say "All right, all right, recess time." Médor loved my grandmother, I said to Madeleine. Whenever the fancy took him he would cross the forest by himself. He never got lost. Sometimes from far away he would spot my grandfather on his way to visit us. Knowing that my grandfather would take him home, Médor would hide among the trees. An easy thing to do for him in winter when there was snow everywhere, but not in the summertime. Médor's big white rump would always show between the trees. Poor Médor.

I wanted to tell Madeleine about Solange. But I did not.

"Where is Médor?" Madeleine wanted to know.

"Went to the enchanted forest that beastly summer. Never came back."

Why did I say that? It was not what had happened. Why, when I said it, we had just walked by the place where Médor was buried.

Before I knew it, we were on our way to the forest, Madeleine and I.

We climbed the hill out of the village, we passed the last houses strung along the gravel road and the meadows where cows grazed. Then we were in the poplar grove at the foot of the last hill before the forest. We sat down side by side to rest in the shade of the trees. Poplars have gray-white trunks and silver-lined leaves that rustle even when there is no wind. I had always been with my grandfather when passing the poplar grove. With Madeleine beside me, I shuddered a little. It was getting cold. Soon night would be falling. I thought of the cats coming home for their supper in the warm kitchen. I thought of Médor. Médor.

Madeleine had gotten to her feet. She stood, pale against a pale tree trunk. Then she started towards the road. She turned back and gestured for me to follow her. I slowly got to my feet, knowing I was not going to follow her. She too must have known. She did not wait. She began to walk uphill, not on the road but by the wayside. Her dress and hair blended with the sun-bleached wildflowers.

Halfway up the hill, Madeleine turned back, gestured again towards me. This time, she was waving good-bye.

The top of the hill had been cut to let the road pass before taking a last abrupt turn towards the dark trees. Nothing had grown to cover the layers of raw yellow, ocher, reddish earth that rose straight up above the road. My grandfather had explained to me why the soil had such bright colors. It was stained by minerals and metal oxides. In our area, the soil was stained that way in many places, he had said. Yes, I knew. I remembered where I had seen it before. I would always remember. I wanted to tell my grandfather. But then, I did not.

Madeleine reached the top of the hill. She turned around once more, waved once more, walked on. Her pale blond hair, her washed-out blue dress met with the earth's fiery ochers, reds, and yellows. They vanished as puffs of smoke or dreams vanish. Madeleine never reached the turn in the road.

Down in the poplar grove, silver-lined leaves shivering away, I knew her name had not been Madeleine.

Disparu

Way up on the wall of the girls' schoolroom hung the map of France, a nearly perfect pink hexagon with a black smear at the upper righthand angle in lieu of Alsace-Lorraine, the birthplace of Joan of Arc.

I owned an Alsatian doll, gorgeous in her billowing red skirt and the giant black bow that framed her face, and a Lorraine doll, dainty in a lace bonnet, flowered apron, and fichu.

The two dolls stood for years on the mantelpiece in the dining room—reminders, not toys.

It had taken a thousand years to shape the map of France. Kings had sacrificed their sons on battlefields and married off their hapless daughters to acquire bits of land until the natural borders of mountains, seas, and rivers had been reached.

I knew the map of France had to be made entirely pink again. Everybody knew it. I did not know—did anybody know?—that it would take the blood of Odette's father and the blood of millions of fathers to make the whole map of France pink again.

Some fifty girls aged six to fourteen sat in a classroom big enough for thirty-five. The older girls played at being the teacher's helpers. The teacher was new, a very young woman who had volunteered during the war—"She has no training and no experience whatsoever," my father had said.

Before that day I had not attended school regularly. The harassed teachers had never paid much attention to me.

"My daughter knows nothing, nothing at all," my father had told the teacher the morning I entered school. And so, although an eight-year-old, I sat with the six-year-olds at one of the smallest tables.

On the first morning, half a dozen of us stood around the teacher. We held a first reader opened at page one. Letter A.

I began at once to turn the pages. I was interested only in the simple sentences at the bottom of each page.

"Page one," the teacher told me, "you cannot read that."

"Yes, I can."

"All right, read what is at the bottom of the last page."

I read without difficulty.

At lunchtime the teacher ran down the hill, passing me on my way home. She came to a stop in front of our gate. My father was in the yard.

"Monsieur, monsieur, your daughter can read!" she shouted.

"You don't say!" my father laughed. He did not believe her.

I don't know how I learned to read. No one else ever knew either. I remember staring at a text under the pictures of a gruesome fairy tale once, wishing hard I could read it since nobody had time to read to me. Maybe hard wishing had done it.

I was moved up to the next grade. The tables were bigger. I was closer to Odette. Still forbidden to talk to each other, we exchanged messages on bits of paper, lines and crosses mostly, but they had secret meanings. At recess we played at bumping into each other and jumping back with screams of mock horror.

We rarely met after school. Whenever I was sent on errands I was under strict orders to come home without delay. I did.

I did not like our village streets any longer. They had filled up with people I did not know. Most of them wore shabby clothes. We children looked up at them with suspicion. We also looked up with suspicion at tall Canadian soldiers with clean-shaven faces and neat khaki uniforms. Homesick and often drunk, they tossed coins to us.

Why? We were not begging. The uhlans too had pressed coins into my grandmother's hands when she was a little girl a long, long time before. Is that perhaps something all soldiers do whether they are friends or enemies?

All the houses, no matter how old, were now inhabited. Even a chateau at the far end of Main Street, empty for longer than anyone could remember, its park grown wild, its many windows boarded up, was now occupied. The German prisoners of war and their guards were lodged there.

Mornings and evenings the long rows of sad men in dirty field gray and their armed guards in "horizon" blue made their way to the forest to work. They passed the schools twice a day.

We never tired of staring at them. Some of us had fathers, and I had an uncle, who were prisoners of war in Germany.

Daydreaming was not always enough to fill the long, boring school days. Two weeks or so before Christmas I began to write—rewrite, rather—a story about a Christmas tree by Hans Christian Andersen. I had found the author's name enchanting but his story most unsatisfactory.

I have forgotten my own version, but I remember the small notebook I was writing on, its sad grayish war paper and its brave pink cover of rough cardboard. My father had given me that notebook, the envy of the other children.

I was writing in my lap, in class, so absorbed in my task I did not see the teacher observing me. I did not see her rushing down the podium steps and pouncing on me. Suddenly, my pink notebook was in her hand. She held it up for everybody to see as she stalked toward the monstrous black stove in the center of the classroom. She lifted the stove cover with a poker. Greedy yellow and red flames shot out, singeing my pink notebook before it was delivered to them.

Not one word had been spoken. I could not have protested, I had turned into stone. What I had done must have been very, very bad to deserve such a sudden, severe, wordless punishment.

It took some years before I got the urge to write—or rewrite—another story.

Marie arrived on a cold spring day. She wore no coat, just a school smock. She carried no luggage, not even a bundle. She was my age and about my size. She had black hair and a very white face. She would stay with us until her family could be found, my father said. She had an eye disease that had been caused by fright, my mother said. Nobody would tell me what had frightened her and Marie herself could not remember. Her eyes were bandaged most of the time. Sunlight was dangerous for them.

After a while, my eyes became inflamed and I too was stumbling around blindfolded. The house was kept in semidarkness. Shutters remained closed during the day. At night the dim kerosene lamps were dimmed some more.

At the table our bandages were lifted a little so that we could see the food on our plates. Marie ate any food given to her. I did not. I often tried to shove my meat onto Marie's plate, which irritated my mother.

I don't know what kind of eye disease we had. I don't think anybody ever knew.

Marie went away one day, holding hands with an old man. She carried a doll like the one I had been given and wore a dress just like mine. My mother had made it for her. Her grandfather had been found, my father said.

I have called her Marie here perhaps because I never had a friend called Marie. To tell the truth, I could never remember her real name. She walked into my life and stepped out of it a nameless shadow.

I don't remember the name of the soldier we adopted either.

For some time I had observed my mother making brick-shaped packages as the village women did. She weighed the packages on the scale that my father kept in a glass cabinet in his classroom.

She was sending the packages to the front for a soldier we did not know, she told me.

"A soldier who has become a war orphan, so to say," my father explained. "We have adopted him. His family, his wife and little girl got . . . lost. He is our soldier now. He will spend his furloughs with us. We are sending him packages and letters. You will write to him, won't you?"

Yes, I would write to the orphan soldier and I would save my snacks for his packages.

"What has happened to his wife and little girl?" I wanted to know. "Did they get lost in the forest?"

I badgered my father until he told me that they had disappeared during a bombardment that had entirely destroyed their village.

How could one disappear? Completely disappear? My father could not explain. Could one get blown to pieces so small that nothing could ever be found, not even a bit of ribbon?

Our soldier came on furlough. He was my father's age. He looked very tired and very sad. My parents kept urging me to go to him, talk to him, go for walks with him. I kept thinking of his wife and little girl. I could not believe that to have me around could make him happy. He seemed so sad whenever he looked down at me and tried to smile.

I never knew whether it was our soldier who brought with him the grown-ups' ghosts that stalk children. But one day they were in the house. And they had come to stay.

The tall dead soldier, standing upright like a pillar holding up the trench wall, lowering his right arm one midnight, has kept his place in my memory. And so has the wounded young soldier hanging in the barbed wire, calling for his mother. And so have the executed —every tenth man shot as a punishment for a battalion's disobedience—the innocent, the brave, the good, as chance would have it.

To the children, ghosts are unforgiving.

The whole of life, at times, was like a bad dream.

"Go home, hurry, your mother is very ill," the teacher told me one day.

I ran straight to my mother's bedroom. I was not often permitted into my mother's beautiful bedroom. The carved bed and dresser there were made of a wood so smooth I always wanted to caress it. The green and pink rug was so pretty I had to take off my shoes to walk on it.

My mother was lying in her big bed propped on embroidered white pillows. My father stood at the foot of the bed with my grandmother, who had just arrived, having crossed the forest on foot all by herself.

My mother gestured for me to come closer. She spoke in a weak voice. She was going to die, she told me. She said something else I did not understand. I was crying. She closed her eyes.

"Go away," she whispered.

My father led me out of the bedroom.

"Your mother is not well, that much is true," he said, "but she is not going to die. I promise you, she is not going to die."

But my mother kept to her bed and refused to talk to my father, my grandmother, or me.

The young teacher came to visit her. She chatted with her. The black-bearded doctor came, and also another doctor who everybody said was a drunkard. She spoke with them.

Then my grandfather came. My mother got out of bed, put on a nice dress, sat at the table, ate, talked, smiled. She was well again.

We all rejoiced.

My grandfather left. My mother turned sad and stopped talking again. Whenever she looked at us it was with eyes that did not see.

"You are not strong enough," I heard my grandfather tell my father. "You have got to be stronger. You have got to force yourself. She needs a strong man. . . . "

My grandfather was a strong man. I felt strong whenever I walked through his nice town, my hand cradled in his big rough hand.

He had dark hair and blue eyes that flashed easily in mirth or anger. His clean-shaven cheeks had a purple hue.

He wore, weekdays and Sundays, ample mason pants of strong corduroy washed to a cream color. I liked the little *swish-swish* they made when he walked.

From the smartly dressed baron and the tall priest in his black robes down to the shabby street sweeper, everyone greeted my grandfather, smiled, or stopped for a chat.

My grandfather had repaired the houses of people too poor to pay, my grandmother had told me. He was forever working on the baron's chateau and he had rebuilt the church steeple. He also had, once, thrown a priest out of his house—a long, long time before, when my mother had been a young girl very ill with typhoid fever.

"Do not come to visit my daughter, please," my grandfather had told the priest. "She will think she is going to die if she sees you at her bedside."

The priest had come anyway. My strong grandfather grabbed him by the shoulders and threw him out of his house.

I heard my mother tell the story many times.

"It was as if my father had thrown death itself out of the house," she always said. "I recovered in no time at all after that."

And, as she also said, it had been lucky that her father had taken things in hand. Only from having seen the priest's black hat lying on her red coverlet for less than a minute, she had, for years to come, dreamed of watching her own funeral.

My mother still needed her father more than she needed us.

The black-bearded doctor came one day with news about a doctor, a specialist, who had discovered a way of treating patients like my mother: hydrotherapy, electricity, counseling . . . My mother revived when she heard about this.

Shortly after, my mother and I were on our way to a southern town where the specialist had an expensive hospital. We could not afford to stay there, and so we took up lodgings in a private home, did our own cooking and, every morning, walked to the hospital.

I spent most of my time waiting for my mother in the hospital park—a beautiful park with great trees, flower beds, lawns, sandy paths, and gardeners at work all the time. Well-dressed ladies who did not look very sick sat in wicker chairs and occupied themselves doing embroideries between treatments. My mother did the same. She had animated talks with the other ladies about ailments, treatments, diets, and about the doctor. They never tired of praising the doctor.

At the end of a week, the doctor told my mother that he wanted to talk to my father. My father came to see the doctor. A few days later we all went home.

My father told me many years later what the famous doctor's laconic diagnosis had been: "Digestive tract damaged by typhoid fever. Diet I prescribed should take care of that. Healthy, strong woman. A baby every other year would not bother her at all. I advise a baby. And please take your wife home."

My mother came home with a new faith: the Proper Diet. She had brought back from her trip the books of a certain Dr. Carton. She read and reread them, told everybody about them, and put the whole family on a diet.

"Red meat, butter, and sugar ruin our health," wrote Dr. Carton. Red meat, butter, and sugar were banished from our table. Which was rather convenient at the time.

"The French would grow taller by three centimeters in two generations if they could only renounce their unhealthy breakfast," Dr. Carton wrote. My mother at last approved of the odd breakfast my grandmother had devised for me: leftover soup from the evening meal—a smooth mixture of vegetables and grain I loved, instead of the coffee and boiled milk that had made me sick.

One spring morning my father hoisted on the right side of the big clock on City Hall's roof a flag that had the same colors as the French flag but was more festive with its red and white stripes and its cluster of stars.

My father had hoisted other flags whenever a victory had been won by our allies, but no other flag waving on City Hall's roof had ever made so many people happy.

My father, my grandfather, and the mayor stood in the yard looking up at the flag waving in the blue sky. They smiled and agreed on everything they talked about that day. My mother came out of the house and joined them. A very unusual thing for her to do. Later, my father and I realized it had been on that very day that her health had finally begun to improve.

In early summer, news came that a train loaded with American soldiers would make a stop at some railroad station not too far away.

We got up before dawn, my father, my mother, and I, plucked up all the flowers in our garden, and climbed on our bicycles.

We waited on a platform with other people who also carried flowers. The train arrived in billows of smoke. My father held me in his arms and I offered my flowers to the tall, clean-shaven Americans in their khaki uniforms. They were many. And I had only one bunch of flowers. I undid the bunch and put one flower in every one of the hands I could reach. This made the Americans laugh. They gave me flat, bland biscuits that I liked much better than the sweet ones I knew. I kept one in a tin box tucked away in a corner of the dining room dresser for a long time.

Nearly half a century later, I met an American gentleman who, when a young soldier bound for the French front during World War I, had exchanged a biscuit for a flower at some small railroad station in France. We did not recognize each other, but we wondered.

My mother was again cooking meals for the schoolchildren, and she had even taken over one of my father's numerous duties. Every Saturday she was delivering the food vouchers to the village poor. I always accompanied her.

The vouchers were small squares of paper, signed and stamped by the mayor, on which my father had written: "Good for one kilogram of meat."

"Nearly three hundred years have passed since Good King Henry promised us one hen in every pot every Sunday," my father once said. "We indeed have made great progress in three hundred years!"

My father made fun of many things, and I did not always understand why. The people to whom we brought the vouchers always thanked us. A very old man who had been a sea captain in the South Seas and now lived in a little house filled with strange masks and artifacts often gave me presents—a tiny vase, a picture, or a fan.

Our task was not always easy. Many of the poor lived far out. To reach them we had to walk for hours through fields and woods.

One evening we were attacked by a big dog. My mother threw stones at the dog and finally chased him away with a stick. Nothing happened to me, but her dress was badly torn.

The dog's owners, a woman and two children, were desolate over the incident.

"That's nothing," my mother told them, "nothing at all, I assure you."

And she even explained to the woman how she was going to pull threads from her dress's seams and mend the tear with them. She would make an invisible mending, she said.

That was how my mother was. She could get upset about trifles (I had seen her faint over a broken cup once) and could also be brave in the face of real danger and gracious about irreparable damage. She could not replace a good wool dress during the war, she knew that.

Our soldier came on furlough again. He was still sad and tired.

"The Americans are going to put an end to the war," my father told him.

Our soldier shook his head sadly. He did not believe that.

My mother cooked the best meals for him. She even baked a pie.

My father took a photograph of him holding me by the hand the morning he returned to the front.

Only a few weeks later, my father received a letter that he held for a long time before he opened it.

Disparu—disappeared—missing, it said in the letter. Our soldier, like his wife and his little girl, was missing. *Disparu*.

If only I had been able to imagine our missing soldier meeting, somewhere, in the peace of a sky forever blue, his missing wife and his missing little girl . . . But I had not been taught to believe in this kind of afterlife. My losses would always be without remedy.

In the middle of winter, my father obtained a special permission to have me in his classroom. He never told me how. This intrigued me even then, but mostly it gave me a feeling of being protected and important.

I had no trouble switching schools. I had watched the boys play from our kitchen window during all those years I had been either too young or too ill to attend school. On my good days I had even sat in my father's classroom for short periods of time. The orderly boys' school could not be as bewildering as the noisy, untidy girls' school and its harassed teacher had been. Solange was dead and I was forbidden to talk to Odette. The other girls shunned me—because I was the teacher's daughter and they were farmers' and shopkeepers' daughters, I guess. Anyway, I was not good at playing their quaint games, and I knew it.

The boys were playing war games. They built trenches in the snow, crouched in them, pelting each other with horse chestnuts and exterminating enemies by the thousand. I was eager to join, but to my sorrow and anger they turned me down as a soldier. I could

The orphan soldier and the author.

be a Red Cross nurse, they said, but not a soldier. Being the teacher's daughter did not help. Even after I procured old umbrellas found in the attic that they turned into machine guns, they refused to let me shoot.

I had my day, once. I persuaded the boys to put on a play: *Joan of Arc*, with me as Joan of Arc. While on the scaffold, I broke my chains, pounced on the gawking German soldiers, and set them on fire. Even older boys who knew better had agreed to have the Germans burn Joan of Arc, not the British.

We did not hear the big guns rumbling any longer. But bombs had fallen on the streets of Paris and even on the streets of Chartres. I knew Chartres. Great-aunt Ernestine lived there.

The bombs had been dropped from airplanes. "What is that, an airplane?" I wanted to know.

"You should know," my mother said. "We took you to an air show once. We kept telling you to look up at the airplane. You would not. You were interested only in a mole that had just popped out of its burrow!"

I remembered. I also remembered a well-dressed gentleman, his straw hat, black-and-white-striped trousers, and cane. He had killed the mole with that cane.

"You attacked him, you grabbed his cane," my mother said.

"Yes, I did." I was still indignant.

"Well," my mother said, "we saw the airplanes, you did not."

My mother was teasing me. That was good. She was not ill any longer. She assured me my grandfather would show me pictures of airplanes. He did.

One day my grandfather came up with an intriguing story. My great-aunt Berthe, who lived in the same town as my grandfather, had lost all her savings "in the Russian railroads," he said.

My great-aunt Berthe was a businesswoman who had sold cheese, butter, and eggs all her life and had been very good at it. How could she have put all her money on a train bound for the faraway, unknown, and no doubt treacherous snows of Russia? This was so odd it made me laugh. My father also laughed.

"If it were only Aunt Berthe's money," my grandfather said, "I would laugh too. But it is far more serious than that." My grandfather was irritated with the two of us, I could tell.

Then the talk turned to the revolution in Russia and, as my grandfather said, that was no laughing matter either. The revolution in Russia was a mystery to me. The only thing I knew for sure was that it did not make my father unhappy but it did make my grandfather unhappy.

Whenever these two disagreed, I was in trouble. I could never decide which side to take. And they often disagreed these days. My father read one newspaper. My grandfather read his own newspaper and also my father's. The two newspapers, I understood, expressed different views on many important happenings.

"If you listen to only one bell," my grandfather said gruffly, "you hear only one sound."

And now my father was turning against the generals who led our armies. I liked the old generals. There were pictures of them hanging on the walls in our house and in all the houses I knew. I liked their white mustaches and their embroidered kepis. They were the stern old men, the grandfathers, the protectors.

I could not understand my father. The newspapers, in giant letters, reported the victories of our armies. Generals led armies to victory, I knew that from the pictures I had seen in our history books.

One Sunday afternoon as I entered the dining room, I saw my father taking down from the wall a framed picture of General Joffre. I stood by the door. "Who shoots the soldiers who have disobeyed orders? The generals?" I asked.

My father turned around and sat down on a chair, holding the picture in his lap.

"No," he said.

"Who shoots them?"

"The soldiers who obey orders shoot the soldiers who disobey, I guess," my father said.

He hung the picture back on the wall. He took my hand and we went out together.

The trees were green. Birds were chirping. It was summer. This is, I think, the only time I walked on the village streets holding hands with my father. We greeted an old man. A dog barked. The village was very quiet. We passed Odette's house.

"Why did Odette's father have to die?" I asked.

"I don't know," my father said. "I don't know."

Then after a while he said, "There are terrible questions that have no good answers."

That did not explain anything but was somehow soothing, in a sad way.

Then our turn came. People at home began to get sick and die. A new calamity was stalking the land: influenza.

My grandmother became so ill we had to go visit her very suddenly. I was taken out of bed before dawn one morning and bundled up in blankets. A farmer took us, my father, my mother, and me, across the forest by horse and buggy. We found my grandmother in bed. She was very pale and could hardly talk. My grandfather led me out of the bedroom and sat with me in the kitchen. Then the farmer took us home.

Soon after, my grandfather wrote that my grandmother was recovering but that he had become ill. He ordered us to stay home and not come to visit him. He was going to be all right, he wrote.

By that time I was also sick. I remember lying on a cot in the kitchen. My father would rush from his class to give me warm tea or soup and then rush up the stairs to my mother, who was also sick.

My father, miraculously, did not get sick. Or maybe he did and nobody knew.

We recovered eventually. Many people of our village were less lucky than we were.

And then the eleventh of November 1918 was upon us.

I remember nothing of the day that marked the end of a long nightmare and brought about wild rejoicing in half the world. Nothing. The joyful memory of Armistice Day 1918 has been, for me, erased by the memory of its yearly solemn, mournful commemorations.

These I remember only too well. They took place under a sad sky and cold drizzle. Always. In separate groups schoolboys and schoolgirls and their teachers walked in procession to the unknown soldier's monument and gathered in back of it. Erected at the graveyard's upper corner, near the tall cross, it consisted of a white stele bearing a bronze plaque on which the names of the village's fallen soldiers were engraved in gold. For reasons I could never comprehend, six large, well-polished artillery shells, linked by a brass chain, had been set around the stele. An unknown soldier lay buried under the stele. For me, the unknown soldier was Odette's father.

The ceremonies began with us children singing *The Marseillaise*—out of tune. The village grown-ups, in mourning, silently stood facing us. The mayor and the adjunct to the mayor made speeches. And then I— always I—stepped forward to the front of the stele, and recited a poem picked out by my father. A poet, whose name I have forgotten, through my trembling voice urged, begged, ordered the ones who want to fight wars to forgo victory parades and take a walk on a battlefield at the hour the crows descend upon it.

A Dream's Grave

Two weeks and two days after the armistice, my father woke me one morning early.

"Get up! Go to your mother, she has a surprise for you."

My mother was asleep. I walked around her bed on tiptoes. A village woman, who often came to help, sat on a low chair in front of the fireplace. She held a bundle wrapped in a white blanket across her broad lap. She opened the blanket and removed swaddles.

"Look," she said, "look at your baby sister!"

I saw a sausagelike reddish body, tiny struggling limbs, a round head with wispy black hair, opaque eyes, and a mouth agape in either despair or anger.

"She surely picked a windy night to arrive! And before the doctor showed up, too," the woman laughed. "A beautiful baby she is, beautiful . . . "

I gingerly kissed my baby sister on her forehead. I could not say a word. I was thinking of all the newborn animals I had seen: puppies, kittens, baby rabbits, guinea pigs, mice . . . They all had been cuddly and cute. None of them had made such distressing sounds.

A beautiful baby? I thought about that the whole day long.

That evening, I sat by myself at the kitchen table doing my homework. The November wind was whistling and howling through the cellar's narrow windows and all the chimneys in the house. Shuddering a little, I listened to the wind's weird music. Suddenly, mixed with it, I perceived cries, baby cries almost, coming from the outside by the front door, of all places.

I rushed through the dark entrance hall and opened the heavy door halfway. A gust of cold wind whipped my face, and a shadow with fiery eyes brushed against my legs and shot straight into the kitchen.

I followed, closing all the doors behind me. I found myself face to face with the biggest, the most beautiful black-and-gray-striped cat I had ever seen.

I retreated behind the kitchen table.

The cat, keeping hypnotic green eyes on me, flattening himself against the wall, inched toward the back of the kitchen, where our two calico cats were having their supper.

As if expecting him, our cats made room for the newcomer. Then they sat back, licked one front paw each, and wiped clean whiskers and ears, indicating they were through with their meal. (I did not know then it was a cat's custom to let bums eat their supper.)

The handsome bum licked the plates clean. He did not take time to wash up, but directed a green look at me and slunk to the door.

I went to open it on tiptoes. He slipped into the dark hall and turned into a shadow again. I opened the entrance door for him. He flew back into the night on a gust of wind.

My grandfather came the next day. I rushed to meet him.

"Guess what . . . the whirlwind brought me a baby sister!" I said.

We looked at each other and burst into a laugh. My grandfather had been the first to guess when I had stopped believing in Santa Claus.

"And the whirlwind brought me a great big cat also."

"A cat?"

"A beautiful cat, much, much more beautiful than . . . " I stopped short.

"She will turn into a beautiful baby, you will see." My grandfather smiled.

He walked up the stairs to my mother's bedroom.

Every evening I waited for the cat to come again. He did, but not every day. He seemed to know at what time, exactly, we served supper to our cats. One snowy evening he consented to stay overnight, and my father and I knew we had acquired a new cat. We named him Toto—the name we gave to all male black-and-gray-striped cats in my family.

Soon, Toto sat by the fire, curled up on chairs, and purred like any other cat. He also found his way to my bed, the only cat in the house to do so. By Christmas we were going to sleep nose to nose every night.

Before retiring, my father would pick up Toto from my bed and take him to the attic. In the morning I would fetch him.

It was easy and fun to go the attic. In the guest room closet, behind my mother's great wedding dress that hung there, a low door and a flight of stairs led to the vast upper room that stretched all the way over City Hall and the girls' school.

A sparse light and sometimes a bit of sun fell from narrow skylights. It was cold there except during the summer months, when it was too hot. Neither cold nor heat could keep the cats or me from exploring the attic. It was full of treasures.

Right by the door stood the firemen's discarded musical instruments, big and small horns agape, brass agleam, ready to shatter the silence. Hundreds of music sheets lying around served as beds for the cats.

There was a trunk filled with ancient clothes. A long, tan satin dress adorned with tarnished gold lace and another of brittle crimson taffeta were the most beautiful dresses I had ever seen. Sachets of potpourri that had lost all aroma were pinned to their under-skirts. I could never bring myself to put on these dresses for the acrid and musty smell they gave out. Toto too turned up his nose at them. But I strutted in a long black cape that had a purple chatoyant silk lining and was brand new.

With tools I was not permitted to use, I pried open the rusty lock of a leather trunk that had been pushed under the eaves.

Toto, sitting close by, watched me out of unmoving eyes.

The trunk was filled with bundles of white old-fashioned hand-embroidered lingerie tied up with faded pink silk ribbons. Sprigs of lavender that had turned odorless and gray were scattered over the lingerie.

I had come upon the trousseau of a girl whose marriage had failed to take place. I had opened a dream's grave. I should not have touched anything, and I knew it. But then, there were lovely handkerchiefs loosely bound together right on top. I pulled one out and unfolded it. It had a wide border of fine lace, and embroidered initials so adorned with curlicues and interlaced with tiny flowers I could not read them at first. I tried hard. Suddenly, I had a jolt; these were my own initials! Or was I mistaken, perhaps? Suddenly I knew I did not want to know. I tried to fold the handkerchief the way I had found it. I could not. I shoved it back under the knotted pink ribbon and slammed down the trunk's heavy lid. I tried to lock up the trunk. I could not—I had broken the lock. I buried it under armfuls of war newspapers my father had stored in a corner.

Near an untidy pile of old leather-bound books chewed up by mice, I spotted a plain brown cardboard box. Its cover was not secured in any way. I had only to lift it, and I had discovered the letters my parents had exchanged before their marriage.

I read the letters. I had to. I could never have resisted my curiosity.

Some were addressed to "Dear Mademoiselle" and "Dear Monsieur," but most to "Dear Geneviève" and "Dear Gabriel." We were not supposed to know our parents' first names in those days. I could make believe I did not know Geneviève and Gabriel when they stepped out of yellowing pages kept in a cardboard box in the attic. And these were legendary names too. A Saint Geneviève had defended Paris against the Vikings one thousand years before, and there had been—or there was—an archangel Gabriel, whatever an archangel was.

Geneviève, in her shapely handwriting, wrote short, easy-to-read letters that told very little. Except once. "The other day," she wrote, "we were working on a wedding dress." (Geneviève was one of the apprentices in a dressmaker's shop.) "All the girls cut off a curl of their hair and enclosed it into the wedding dress's hem. 'It's a charm and it works in case you want to get married before the end of the year,' the silly girls told me." Nowhere did Geneviève say whether she too had enclosed a curl of her hair. She held back her secrets.

Gabriel's letters were long and hard to read. He wrote very fast about his pupils, his jovial school director, and people he had met. He wrote whole stories in a witty, kind way. I loved my father's hard-to-decipher love letters.

Would I ever get such letters myself someday?*

When I told my mother that Toto had made his appearance the day my sister had been born, she was delighted.

"This means good luck," she said.

My mother loved cats. And then, most events meant good luck to her, these days. She was well.

---

*Yes, I would. One. Forty years later, from my father. Written in longhand, it is sixty-eight pages long.

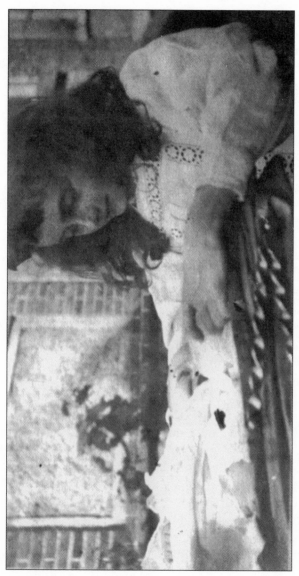

The author and her sister, Elaine.

Toto became a member of the family. He always remained proud and independent. I never thought of dressing him in dolls' clothes. The girls' schoolteacher, who boasted that she could hypnotize cats, stared at close range into Toto's eyes, once. With one swipe of his paw he sent her eyeglasses flying.

Nothing of that sort ever happened to me. We got along very well, Toto and I.

These were happy days. I had been promoted to big sister status. My little sister had turned into a beautiful baby. My mother had named her Eliane. All the attention had shifted to Eliane, and that was good. I could now go to Odette's house, she could come to mine—nobody paid any attention.

In school I had easily fallen into the new routine. To this day, I remember the schedule of studies in my father's classroom. The six hours a day, five days a week of studies were so diversified and so well distributed they never were a burden. I have completely forgotten my high school and college schedules.

"You have to make up for nearly three lost years," my father often reminded me. "And remember, you have to be ready to take the examination of the *certificat d'études primaires* in only two years."

The dreaded exam, no longer required, was then a sword of Damocles over every child's head. If one could not pass this exam between the ages of twelve and fourteen, the road was forever closed. One could not study any further and consequently would never amount to anything.

I cannot remember whether I took this seriously. Playing with the boys turned out to be more difficult for me than studying. The war games already had been a disappointment. And now, in all the games that involved running, the boys arranged to favor me. Even when we played marbles, I soon realized, they cheated to let me win. Protected, helped, flattered, I was soon abusing my privileges.

We had a slightly retarded boy named Victor in our school. Eager to please me, he would bring me baby animals: rabbits, guinea pigs, even bats. I required a fox. Victor eventually brought me a young fox that his father had caught in the woods. We chained the terrified animal in the empty doghouse. Someone, probably my father, let him loose during the night.

"I'll give you a whole chocolate bar if you bring me a baby wolf," I told Victor. "But if you don't, I'll do something horrible to you."

That same day an older boy came up to me after school.

"I have to talk to you," he said.

Older boys usually did not bother talking to younger children.

"Do you know that Victor is just a poor simpleton?" the older boy asked.

"Well, sure, I know that," I said.

"Good, now listen. Just because you are smarter, and because you are the teacher's daughter, you don't have the right to take advantage of him. Only a coward takes advantage of someone weaker. Do you understand that?"

Coward. This was an ugly word. And a powerful one too. I tried it a few evenings later on two big boys I saw stoning a toad in a lonely lane.

The toad was ugly, but he was harmless, everybody knew that. And he looked pitiful too. There was a blob of blood near his round golden eyes.

"Cowards! Cowards!" I screamed.

The boys dropped their stones and walked away.

I was a willing learner at age ten, and there was a lot to learn in every field.

One evening, Simon, a boy slightly younger than myself, and I stayed after class to do some homework we had not returned on time.

We hurried to finish our task and started talking. Words and giggles bounced eerily in the vast empty classroom. It was at once intimidating and exciting.

"How come you go to the boys' school?" Simon asked.

"One does not learn anything at the girls' school," I said.

"My sisters go to the girls' school and they learn," Simon said.

And then, we were discussing differences between boys and girls.

"I know more than you do," Simon said. "I have a big brother and two sisters. You have only one baby sister."

I had nothing to say to that.

"I bet you don't even know what a boy looks like," Simon said.

"I have seen baby boys," I said.

"I am not talking about babies, you silly," Simon said.

"All right, tell me . . . " I said.

"Me, I would say," Simon confided, "'it' looks more or less like a little carrot . . . "

I giggled.

Simon was offended. In a loud voice he began: "But my big brother . . . "

The classroom door opened with a clatter and my mother came in.

"Go home," she told Simon, "the teacher is busy."

She glared at me.

I was never again left alone with a boy after school.

I would have been cut off from the girls' world entirely without Odette. With her I sometimes joined the other girls after school. I knew I could not juggle, hopscotch, or jump rope as well as they did. I would never know the songs and dances they knew either. And without Odette I would never have known what happens to girls when they grow up until it had happened to me. She once talked an older girl into showing me her bloodstained white panties.

I asked no question for fear of sounding silly. Anyway, nobody had any explanation. "That is the way it is," Odette said.

I brooded over the revelation. Left to my own devices, no grown-up or book giving any interpretation, I found the unexplained spilled blood perplexing. Was there, perhaps, some mysterious connection with the spilled blood of sacrificial victims in ancient religions? Could it have something to do with death? Or with life? Faced with a mystery, I conceived an obscure reverence for what I was fated to become.

Years later, of course, I would repeat with the smart set that it was a nuisance—a curse, even—to be a woman. I never believed it.

"Eliane is not growing at all anymore," my mother announced one day. She was in a panic.

The black-bearded doctor was summoned.

"Cow's milk," he said, shaking his head. "Cow's milk does not agree with the baby."

My mother, to her great sorrow, had not been permitted to nurse because she had had influenza shortly before Eliane's birth. The only known remedy then was goat's milk.

My father and I roamed the countryside every evening after school until we came home late one night with a beautiful blond goat that kept kicking and boxing our bicycles. By the time spring arrived, baby Eliane, nurtured on uncooked goat-warm milk, had started to grow again.

The village had begun to come back to its old self. The refugees were leaving. Many men had returned.

The German war prisoners had gone and the dilapidated chateau that had housed them was now filled with masons and carpenters. In the chateau's gardens, gardeners were pulling weeds out of flower beds and pruning trees. This made the sleepy village look more drab and neglected than ever.

Articles, signed "A concerned citizen," were appearing in our local newspaper. They told about our trashy public square, the potholes on Main Street, and the splendid nettles flourishing along our graveyard's crumbling walls.

The one-page newspaper was published once a week in the neighboring town and was all over our village every Saturday. The villagers waving it would call on each other and on my father.

"Did you read that one?" "Who could have written it?" They laughed. My father laughed with them.

The mayor and the councillors did not laugh. They were accused of neglecting the village, which indeed was the case. They were offended. They badly wanted to know who this "concerned citizen" was.

I knew who this was.

"As an employee of the government," I had once heard my mother say to my father, "you cannot mix in politics."

"Nonsense!" my father had said. "And besides, nobody will ever know. The editor burns the manuscripts in my presence."

One day, during school hours, an old gentleman in a dark suit and hat entered the classroom. My father greeted him as *Monsieur l'Inspecteur*.

We were sent out into the schoolyard long before recess time. I could tell this was not the routine once-a-year class inspection.

I ran to my mother. She was in the kitchen, holding Eliane in her arms and looking out of the window.

"I knew something was going to happen," she said when I came in.

She was upset.

Suddenly she said, "Go tell your father that the boys have been in recess for almost twenty minutes and nobody is watching them."

"Oh, Mother! . . . "

"Go, I am telling you, go! But knock on the door first."

I did not run. I stood with a pounding heart in front of the classroom door for a good while, then I barged in, forgetting to knock.

The inspector, seated at my father's desk, and my father, standing in front of him, peered down at me.

"Mother said the boys have been playing for thirty minutes and nobody is watching them," I said in a shrill voice.

Did I see a smile on the inspector's face?

"And Victor fell . . . I think," I added. I could feel my face burning. I scurried out, slamming the door behind me.

"You were right," I heard my father tell my mother afterwards, "somebody denounced me for engaging in politics!" He laughed.

"I told you," my mother said. "I told you so!"

For a long time after that, forever maybe, I would be unable to dissociate the word *politics* from trash in the town square, potholes on Main Street, and nettles growing along crumbling graveyard walls.

On one of the first warm days, I saw Toto stalking across the meadow behind the house as if on urgent business. He was heading for the woods that were part of the vast park surrounding the castle. I saw him disappear in the undergrowth. By nightfall he had not come back. I called and called.

"Toto has gone for the summer," my mother said. "He will be back when the weather gets cold."

I was desolate. I wanted to believe my mother. I could not.

And there was more sadness to come.

There would be no festivities to mark the end of the school year. The last *distribution des prix* had taken place in July 1914. Too young to take part, I had only watched. I remembered the stage decorated with green branches where the mayor and the councillors sat. The schoolchildren, one by one, had climbed the steps of the stage. The mayor and the councillors had placed crowns of paper oak leaves on the children's heads and given them big beautiful books that had bright red embossed covers and gilded pages.

The end-of-school festivities would eventually return, after my school days were over. The great red gilded books and the crowns of oak leaves never would.

Then, only two days before the summer vacation started, Odette announced that she would soon be moving away. She was so excited imagining her life in a new place, she forgot everything else. I was hurt.

Odette and her mother came to City Hall to get some documents and say good-bye.

I was so downhearted I could not find anything to say.

"You will visit me and I'll visit you," Odette said. "That will be much more fun than to be living together in the same old village."

Her mother and my parents decided that I would go to spend one whole week at Odette's new home in August.

A few weeks later, in the early morning, my father and I cycled the ten kilometers to the next town and I climbed into the train bound for Paris. I had traveled alone on our little local train, never on such a big train. The people in my compartment promised my father that they would remind me to get out at the right stop.

All went well. The trip was short. I could never have missed the right station. Odette stood on the platform there, waving a white handkerchief. We greeted each other as if years had passed since our last meeting.

We walked on a dirt road along the railroad tracks for half an hour or so and there was Odette's house. Made of gray stucco with brick trimmings around the door and windows, it looked like a tiny railroad station.

I had seen these houses before from the train. They stood at every crossing along the railroad tracks. "Who could be living in them?" I had always wondered.

Whenever a train announced itself, hooting from far away, a long iron gate was rolled across the road to keep people and animals from walking into the path of the train. As soon as the train had passed, the gates would be rolled back.

It was the job of Odette's mother to roll the gates back and forth when the roaring, hooting trains passed by, six times a day, shaking the ground, engulfing everything in billows of smoke.

"The government gave my mother a house and a job because my father was killed in the war. My mother is a war widow and I am a ward of the nation," Odette said.

There was a small garden, a tiny rabbits' hutch, and a barnyard behind the house. The flowers looked sick.

"The trains' smoke is poison for the flowers," Odette said.

There were no neighbors. The village and the school were kilometers away.

"I can't roll those heavy gates yet," Odette said. "But one day I'll be strong enough and I'll roll them, you'll see."

For a week we watched the trains passing by and waved at them all. We walked to town on errands. This was a much bigger town than our old village. The stores were nicer, and the schools much bigger. But one had to walk for over an hour to reach them and carry books and groceries on the way home.

Then the week was over. I went home the way I had come, by myself, on the big train. I felt quite grown up. But, remembering Odette and her mother in their lonely house, rolling iron gates back and forth and waving at the trains that rattled the cups in their cupboard and spewed poison on their flowers, I felt sad.

In September, Odette came to spend a week with me. She wanted to do everything she had done before leaving the village, she said.

Every evening we fetched the milk at the farm and let the cat that had followed us drink out of the milk can cover. We danced on the road, holding on one extended hand a wicker basket of cottage cheese while executing fancy arm contortions without spilling one bit, as we had done before. We made fishing poles out of sticks and thread, fishing hooks out of bent pins, and went to fish at the river.

On Sunday, Odette went to mass. I walked along the graveyard wall behind the church and listened to the music a lady made on the harmonium.

Odette took flowers to Solange's grave.

"Somebody has planted forget-me-nots among the daisies," she said, running back. "It makes like a wreath at the head of the grave! Who could have done that? It can't be Léonie. We saw her move away."

I did not think it mattered much who had planted the forget-me-nots, but Odette did. She was still wondering when we peeked over the graveyard wall on the grown-ups' side and remembered where we had seen the will-o'-the-wisp dancing between the graves.

One afternoon we took a walk and ended up at the poplar grove. Now was the time to tell Odette about Madeleine. Odette had told me when she had seen a white form fluttering over Solange's grave.

But just then Odette said, "You know what, my mother is going to remarry!"

And she went on telling me about a man who had come to help with the moving. He was still coming, she said, and bringing fruit and vegetables from his garden.

"He likes my mother, I can tell," she said.

"Do you like him?" I wanted to know.

"Oh, I don't know," Odette said. "A man . . . it's just a man."

I was amazed.

"But I surely hope I'll get a little sister like yours, someday," she laughed.

It got chilly. It always gets chilly under the poplars in September. We decided to go home. I had not told Odette about Madeleine. I would always be good at keeping secrets to myself.

We went to say hello to the goat, who at once stood on her hind legs and showed us her bony head. She had never liked us.

"Don't tease the goat," Odette said. "It could make her milk turn bitter and that would be very bad for the baby."

Odette loved babies. She wanted to carry baby Eliane around. But baby Eliane wanted to be carried around by her mother only.

Odette went home. We would not see each other for one whole year, probably. That was something we could not imagine very well.

We promised to write.

"Write as soon as you know who planted the for-get-me-nots," Odette said as we waved good-bye.

"From now on, school will have to be your only preoccupation," my father told me on the first day of school.

I was not worried. I did as well in school as boys my age, I knew that. Not in mathematics. But that was the rule, was it not? Boys were better than girls in math, I had always been told. Not even my father could make me worry about school. And anyway, there was still a long, long year to go.

On the first cold day of October, as my mother had predicted, Toto returned. The event made up for the sadness that comes with the end of summer. It also gave me a new confidence. There were, after all, a few things that could be predicted in this life.

Eliane was afraid of Toto. But then, she was afraid of everything. Would always be.

My father was now working on a new project.

"Consumers' cooperatives are sprouting all over the country," I had heard him say. "We must get one."

To this day, I cannot understand how he sold this idea to the small farmers in our poor, stony, hilly part of the country. But he did.

The farmers bought shares. Promised a percentage on their future purchases, they patiently waited for the store to open.

My father coaxed the mayor into becoming the president of the future cooperative and the councillors into becoming its administrators. He, of course, would be the volunteer treasurer, secretary, and chief administrator. He would do all the work.

Finding a location for the cooperative was the first problem. No suitable empty store was available in the whole village. There were three tiny grocery stores run as side businesses by three cafés, and a large general store that boasted a telephone and the best location on Main Street and yet was not doing well at all.

The owner, Monsieur Lebon, a good-looking man in his thirties whose cheeks were so red they looked painted, always greeted his customers with a sad, frozen grin.

"He drinks," people said behind his back.

My father approached Monsieur Lebon. A deal was concluded. The general store had been acquired by the cooperative and Monsieur Lebon had become its manager.

Glossy green paint replaced the peeled-off gray on the store's facade, the empty shelves filled up with merchandise, and a broad smile replaced the sad, frozen grin on Monsieur Lebon's face.

At the far end of the village, the chateau that had housed the German prisoners had become The Nest in the Woods, a home for orphans and the women who took care of them. It was now a bright-green-and-white residence, at odds with the village houses, their walls of patched-up stucco, their rickety gray shutters and dark slate roofs.

The orphans, both boys and girls, wore pretty light beige capes with pointed hoods over their red-and-white-checked smocks. They marched in orderly rows, singing, down the village streets where not long ago the prisoners of war had marched.

With the village children, I watched in amazement. As an older girl said, "These are orphans—why do they look so pretty and so happy?"

The director of The Nest in the Woods came to visit at City Hall. He was a tall, slim, well-dressed gentleman with smiling blue eyes and dark wavy hair. He had an unusual name—Bertrand-Kapp. Soon everybody was calling him Monsieur Bertrand.

Monsieur Bertrand and my father got along the first time they met. Soon they were doing business. The orphanage needed groceries. The cooperative would provide them.

On occasion, I would listen to my soft-spoken father and the distinguished Monsieur Bertrand haggling over the price of a bag of beans, sugar, or rice. They were fierce. I could not believe my ears. It took me some time to understand why these two men could allow themselves to be so ruthless; they were not fighting for themselves but for their own creations.

"If your father were in business for himself," my mother's father once said to me with some bitterness, "you would be rich."

Pretty little Eliane could walk now. I took her along on errands. Everybody admired her.

We went to get milk at the farm in the evening. One of our cats always followed us, sat behind a rock near the farm's gates waiting to lap the warm milk I would pour for him into the milk-can cover. Eliane watched with great interest.

"Is it true you are letting the cat drink out of the milk-can cover?" my mother asked one day.

Before I had time to say anything she said, "Don't lie, Eliane told me."

Eliane could speak only three words, but she could already tell on me. She had an uncanny sense of what I should not do, whether it was snatching a cookie, juggling with buns, or dancing on the street while balancing a basket of cottage cheese on one hand.

My mother loved it. She would tell everybody about Eliane's extraordinary skills as a watchdog.

One day, Monsieur Bertrand invited me to spend the Sunday afternoons with the children at the orphanage. I was delighted.

The long walks and the picnics in the woods with the children were very nice. Yet, I did not feel at ease.

There I was, a child who possessed everything, among children who possessed nothing except each other's company. They seemed quite happy as far as I could see, and they did not mind me either. Still, I was not one of them.

When the weather was bad, we played games indoors. One rainy afternoon, two boys, a girl, and I started a gambling game. We had always used beans before, but that day, my partners, who were slightly younger than I was, decided to use real money. Their money consisted of found coins they called their lucky coins, and some silver pieces inherited from a dying parent. The coins in my pocket did not have the special value theirs had.

As luck would have it, I won all the children's lucky coins and inherited silver pieces. The children looked at me. There was utter amazement in their eyes. And perhaps fear. I was stunned, embarrassed, ashamed.

I hurried to suggest another game, which consisted in juggling coins in my closed hands and having the others guess the amount. We played until I had lost all my gains and more.

After that, and for a long time, I regarded money with suspicion. As if it possessed a power of its own that could guide it out of unlucky hands into luckier ones. When some time later I overheard Monsieur Bertrand tell my father that, in his opinion, money was a source of evil, I was more than ready to believe him.

Monsieur Bertrand wanted to do away with money, taxes, and government, my father said one day.

"He is an anarchist!" my mother said angrily.

"Yes, he is," my father said, and he smiled.

"Weren't anarchists men who threw bombs?" I wondered to myself.

My father and Monsieur Bertrand went to Chartres on business.

"We had a lot to do," my father told us when he returned, "but we stopped at the cathedral anyway. The great organ was playing. Monsieur Bertrand jotted down musical notes on the back of an envelope. Back home, the first thing he did was to play the tune he had noted on the piano. Then he started composing a song for the children!

"Not bad for an anarchist!" my father said, and laughed.

Monsieur Bertrand taught songs and plays to the children. For Christmas he put up a glittering tree that reached to the ceiling in the former chateau's grand salon, now a children's playroom. He showed a movie about nature and a Charlie Chaplin movie every Sunday night.

To accompany the silent movies, a shy lady with frizzly hair played the piano. She made a music that had little in common with the firemen's trumpeting, the bellowings of the church's harmonium, or my violin's screeches. It was real music, I guessed.

I wrote Odette a long letter about The Nest in the Woods. No answer came. Odette had expected me to write about the forget-me-nots on Solange's grave, probably. I had not even tried to find out who had planted them. I was not forgetting Solange. I was not forgetting anybody or anything. But something new was happening every day. Life was carrying me away from the past, like a river. I felt vaguely guilty, but helpless.

My father was experiencing difficulties with the co-operative. Complaints were made every day about bottles of rum having been tampered with. The metal caps showed signs of having been removed, then put back into place. And the bottle contents, according to the village experts, had lost their original taste and aroma.

The culprit was easy to find. Monsieur Lebon, this was common knowledge, had always been only too fond of rum.

The cooperative administrative council was summoned. The council met at City Hall on a Sunday afternoon and turned itself into a tribunal. All the cooperative members were invited. I sat in the back, knowing very well I had no business being there.

I watched my father, the accuser. He was deathly pale and his voice was hoarse. Monsieur Lebon, his red face blotched, stood gesturing helplessly, a drunken and doomed man.

Declared an unworthy manager, Monsieur Lebon was dismissed. Shortly after, now dispossessed and jobless, he moved out of the village. It was in April, I remember, the week Toto left for the summer.

Monsieur Lebon's fate disturbed me. I had always known him in his store as a distracted but kind man. I knew he had often given treats to poor children. I remembered how he had, years before, cranked up the phone and pushed a crate in front of it so that I could talk to the doctor when my mother had become ill.

Even if he was a drunk and a bad businessman and manager, I thought, Monsieur Lebon belonged in the big store on Main Street.

I never discussed any of this with my father. I have never found peace about it either.

Maybe it is the unhappiness I felt at the time that drove me to take revenge on the expensive contraption my mother had bought for me from a special mail-order catalog. The thing, made of sturdy beige canvas, equipped with metal plates in the back, was supposed to keep me from stooping by forcing my spine to straighten up when strapped tightly around my abdomen and shoulders. Before dawn one day in May, I gleefully pushed it into a big bucket of soapy water that had been left in the yard. The thing struggled, gurgled, and sent up bubbles. One of the snakelike shoulder straps kept popping out. But finally it too went under. I watched the opaque water calm down, then become perfectly quiet, as if it had nothing to hide.

The cool air, the birds' songs, and the sun freeing itself from a bank of gray clouds were intoxicating that morning.

My mother made herself sick over my misdeed.

Eliane watched me out of uncomprehending, frightened eyes.

"I'll never buy you another corset," my mother said.

Another victory.

The month of June was upon us and the date of the dreaded exam only one month away. I knew I had not worked as hard as I should have. Fear of failing paralyzed me. I could hardly study during the remaining weeks.

On the day of the exam, excitement had replaced fear. Early in the morning, my father and I bicycled to the high school in the next town.

I was all dressed up in a dress of fragile blue voile, net stockings I hated, and patent leather shoes that pinched.

"Don't panic," my father said. "It is just like a long school day."

I filed into a classroom with many other girls. We sat at the usual two-seat tables. The girl who occupied the seat next to mine was at least one head taller than I. She wore a lovely pink dress.

"You'll let me peek, won't you," she whispered.

I looked up at her. She must have been fourteen years old. This was her last chance, I guessed. I winked.

A teacher wrote on the blackboard the text of two arithmetic problems. We copied them and were given thirty minutes to solve them. Then we took a half-page dictation and answered questions in grammar and vocabulary about the dictated text.

After a short recess we had essay writing, then history and geography tests.

The tests in science, drawing, singing, reciting, and sewing took place in the afternoon. The sewing test was the worst: a buttonhole—I had never made one that was not crooked—and the mending of a nasty tear in a piece of snow-white cloth, done with bright red thread.

The girl in the pink dress gave me eau de cologne to rub on my sweaty hands. That was all she could do for me.

We must have had lunch at some time. I don't remember anything about it.

At last—the sun was low on the horizon by then—I stood waiting with my father in a large courtyard among some hundred boys and girls and their parents.

Eventually a teacher appeared at the top of the main building's stairs. He read a list of names.

I listened intently. I did not hear my name.

"Well . . . ," my father said when it was over. He was smiling.

"I didn't pass," I whispered.

"Didn't you hear your name? It was the first one!" my father said.

"The first one?"

I could not believe it.

The girl in the pink dress was waving good-bye from across the street. She was smiling. She had passed, too. I waved back, laughing and clapping my hands.

"Now," my father said, "don't start imagining that you are better than the others. It could be an error, you know. The teachers did not have much time to count points. Or maybe the subjects happened to be just what you knew best. You probably were lucky, for once."

My dear, cautious father, afraid as usual that I would become overconfident! I jumped on my bicycle and rode against the cool evening breeze as if I had been sailing a boat down a great unknown river.

Of Last Things

Very quietly I opened the kitchen door. My grandfather and my mother did not seem to hear me. They were sitting at the upper end of the kitchen table, facing each other under the tall kerosene lamp's shade of green paper lined in yellow and adorned with garlands and ruches that my mother made anew every fall. I saw the twin profiles, caught in a medallion of light, as if for the first time. I had not known how alike they looked.

They went on whispering in a language of their own, gazing at each other and smiling.

"Grandmother died," I said too loudly.

They got to their feet. My grandfather's chair fell on the tile floor with a clatter unseemly in a house just visited by death.

I saw the guilty frown on their faces as they hurried to "her" bedroom.

I walked out into the night, away from them.

They had dared to be happy while my grandmother was dying. That was all I understood then. That was enough.

A judge of thirteen does not have much forgiveness in her heart. I vowed I would never forgive them.

And to punish them right then, I would not tell them what my grandmother's last word had been.

I had received it, I alone, as one receives a thing precious and sacred.

I would tell my father. I would tell Odette, someday. I would tell my grandmother's neighbors, who had so often brought their sick plants to her so that she could nurse them back to health. I might even tell some stranger. Strangers had often stood in front of her gate to admire her hyacinths, tulips, roses, and the wondrous wisteria that was my mother's age, and ran under the eaves the whole length of the house, like a festive garland.

I would never tell them.

My grandmother had suddenly become very ill two evenings before. After a brief examination, the doctor had told us that an artery had burst in her brain. My grandfather and the doctor had looked at each other and said nothing. The doctor had come again in the morning, given my grandmother a shot of morphine, and departed without saying much. All we had done after that was wait. Leaving Eliane with my father, my mother had cycled through the forest and joined us.

I had been by my grandmother's bedside all that day, hoping she would come out of her uneasy sleep, look up at me, talk to me perhaps one last time. But she had not opened her eyes. She had, at times, mumbled words I could not understand. Then suddenly, at sunset, on that dreary March evening, she had said, loud and clear: "Geranium," and she had stopped breathing. A glorious clump of blood-red flowers to send her on her way, another artery bursting.

With my grandmother's death the six happiest months of my life had turned into dead past.

I had been living with my grandparents since September, so that I could keep company to my ailing grandmother, my mother had said.

My father had wanted me to enter high school without delay. Monsieur Bertrand, consulted, had agreed with my father. There was no high school in my grandparents' lovely town. Madame Lemaître, my mother's old teacher, taught a class suitable for girls who would not pursue their studies but had to stay in school until the age of fourteen, which was the law at the time. This was not what I needed, since I was supposed to go on to college. Nevertheless, my mother's decision had prevailed. I was delighted. I knew I would be sent to some faraway boarding school someday. I wanted nothing more than to postpone that day.

My grandmother had been ailing since the dismal spring my mother, then aged sixteen, had been deathly ill with typhoid fever. My grandmother had cared for her day and night. Then she herself had come down with a catarrh that was never cured. It had happened so long before, we all had become used to my grandmother being ill and yet struggling along as if she were not. She would spend her nights propped up on pillows to ease her coughing. She slept little.

A corner of her large bedroom had been turned into sleeping quarters for me. And that was a blessing; I had nightmares at the time. Spiders my size that I

"The grandmother" (mother's mother). Geranium *was her last word*.

could not run away from because terror paralyzed me ambled towards me almost every night. But my grandmother, tall and slim in her white nightclothes and holding aloft a tiny kerosene lamp, would be there, on time without fail, to stop the monsters.

"There are no spiders, look . . . " she would say. "It was only a dream."

My grandmother and I shared secrets. One of them was that she could not read well. Raised on a farm, the eldest of eleven children, she had not gone to school very often. We decided that I would teach her. We practiced whenever no one was around. We did not tell anybody. My grandfather had the surprise of his life the day he caught her reading his newspaper!

My grandmother told me something that very few people had ever known, she said: the story of her mother, Eugénie d'Orange. (The name alone enchanted me.) When a girl of sixteen, Eugénie had been sent to a convent in England, where she had been supposed to receive a lady's education. Her father, a wealthy horse dealer and farmer, had planned to marry her to some rich, perhaps even noble, man.

Eugénie returned two years later, an accomplished, pretty young lady who lost no time in falling in love with the wrong man—the destitute but handsome shepherd on one of her father's farms. What a scandal! And the marriage had to be hurried, too.

I promised my grandmother I would never tell anybody.

As for my grandfather, he was at the time putting the last touches on a dream house he had built for

Monsieur Blake, an English gentleman who had come to live in our town.

Monsieur Blake had wanted a house like the one he had owned before in the suburbs of London. Among all the builders in town, he had chosen my grandfather. He had brought him pictures, and together they had drawn their own house plans on my grandmother's kitchen table.

The house was built of red bricks and had a terraced roof. It was strikingly at odds with all the other houses around, their sturdy stone walls and their high slate roofs.

"Monsieur Blake's house is not in harmony with the houses of this town," I told my grandfather.

"That's true," my grandfather said, "but it is a lot healthier. Our stone houses have kept humidity, maybe even diseases, in their centuries-old walls."

"I like bricks," my grandfather went on, smiling. "I should hate them, but I like them . . . I was ten when I went to work at the brick factory. There were other boys my age working there too. Our job consisted of carrying the bricks as they came out of the oven and setting them on the ground to cool off. Yes, yes, they were still quite warm. After a while, the only way to get back to the oven was by walking over the tightly packed rows of bricks. We had no shoes! We ran. And fast, too."

He had to tell me more.

"My father, your great-grandfather, was born in the Auvergne, a strange and beautiful area. There are sixteen extinct volcanoes there. Some of them have a black lake as still as a mirror in their craters. But little grows there. It is poor country. When a young man, your great-grandfather wandered off in search of a better place to live. He happened to walk through this town one day, saw a girl he liked, and married her. He had no real profession, but he was clever at buying sheep and goats. Soon he owned a little house. A girl and a boy—me—were born. Then—I must have been eight years old—your great-grandfather became home-sick. One morning, before anyone was awake, he just wandered off. My mother somehow knew he had gone home."

"How far was that?"

"Some four hundred kilometers . . . Well, we waited for him to come back. He did not. So my mother, my sister, and I went to fetch him. Walking, yes, sure."

"How long did it take you?"

"I don't remember. Months, I guess. We had to make a living. We worked on farms along the way. We slept in barns. It was summer. We got good food, better than at home. The farmers liked our story, I guess. We found my father, and he came back with us. Everything was fine for some time. Then he went off again, and again. But then, he would come back by himself. Once, I remember, he returned right on time for Mardi Gras. Everybody made merry and wore masks for the occasion in those days. Your great-grandfather appeared on Main Street, disguised as 'the man-who-does-not-know-whether-he-is-coming-or-going.' He wore two similar masks, one over his face, the other over the back of his head, and wooden shoes that were pointing in both directions, forwards and backwards. He cut a fine figure!"

Every Sunday my grandfather and I cycled to my parents'. I felt a little like a stranger now in my parents' house. My mother and Eliane lived in a world of their own. There was little room left for me there, I could tell.

I mentioned this to my father.

"They don't pay much attention to me either," he said, smiling. "At least your mother's health is good."

I was considered too young to go to my grandmother's burial. My mother did not go either. She had taken to her bed.

I stayed with Eliane at the home of Aunt Berthe, who had not spoken to my grandmother since the spring of 1905, when her nephew, my father, had married my mother. Such a promising young man had, in her opinion, deserved a wealthier bride. Moreover, she had decided it was my grandmother's fault that this marriage she disapproved of had taken place. Consequently, for fifteen years, she had not even greeted my grandmother—who had previously been her friend— whenever they met on the village streets.

But at the news of my grandmother's death, Aunt Berthe rushed to us in tears to offer condolences and help. I did not respond too well to her embrace, but she did not seem to notice. My grandfather's glares did not discourage her either. She insisted she wanted to help. And this is how I came to stay with Eliane at Aunt Berthe's big empty house. Her son and husband were minding her store half a block away, her two daughters went with her to the burial.

Eliane had great fun sliding on her bottom on the waxed floors in the upstairs bedrooms.

I looked coldly at everything in the house. The beds of fine wood, their coverlets of red satin and white lace, the silly knickknacks on the dressers, the gleaming copper pans displayed on the kitchen wall, the doors' shiny fixtures told me all that Aunt Berthe knew. If she knew remorse too, it was a remorse that came too late and had no worth, in my eyes.

Eliane's innocent glee irritated me to no end.

Three days later I became one of the boarders in the small boarding school that Madame Lemaître ran on the side. The entire girls' school, five classes in all, teachers' lodgings, and boarding school were housed in a former chateau, a handsome building adorned with small towers and surrounded by the century-old trees of its private park.

Our dormitory was a vast room under a mansard roof. Our dining room was a cavernous kitchen. The Lemaîtres, their daughters, the ten boarders, and Rose, the maid, took their meals together there. Monsieur Lemaître sat at the head of a long table, his wife on his left, his daughter Nelly on his right. I sat near Nelly, Lily at her mother's side, the other boarders down the table, the youngest at the very end.

Rose refused to sit at the table with us. She used as her eating counter a large summer charcoal stove of pretty blue and white faience that she decorated with tall ceramic pots of honey and vases of flowers.

A black cooking stove that seemed to have been made for giants occupied the back wall of the kitchen-refectory.

Rose had been picked up by Madame Lemaître at an orphanage some ten years before. She did the cleaning, the cooking, and the shopping. She also slept with us in the dormitory. She combed our hair in the morning. She tucked us in our beds every night, which was something that some of us needed badly; I was the oldest of the boarders, the youngest was eight. She did it all out of devotion to the Lemaître family.

There was only a wall between the school's park and my grandfather's garden. On the school side, the wall was low enough to be easily climbed. On my grandfather's side, his house being built downhill, the wall was much higher. The day I moved out of his house, my grandfather put up one of his tall mason ladders against his side of the wall.

Madame Lemaître soon discovered the ladder. She ruled that I would have to ask permission whenever I wanted to visit my grandfather and then go through the gate and walk on the sidewalk like everyone else.

I was now close to Nelly all the time. I sat near her in class and at meals, my bed was close to hers in the dormitory, and we stood side by side at our primitive washing basins. She took me as her confidante.

"Did you notice, I resemble beautiful Queen Victoria," she once told me.

She had found a portrait of young Queen Victoria in our history book. She made me stand with her in front of a mirror, took off the gold-rimmed spectacles that had dug a red furrow into her nose, and pointed at all the similarities she saw between herself and the queen.

I agreed. It was easier than telling her what I saw.

Nelly would ask me to button and unbutton her clothes and fix her hair after it had already been fixed by Rose. Worst of all, she wanted me to tickle her neck while we were studying. It all angered me, but I did not dare refuse.

I was a bit afraid of the Lemaître family.

The two daughters I saw, rightly or wrongly, as spies. Madame Lemaître never missed an opportunity to compare me with my mother, who, she said, had been such a docile, intelligent, and hard-working student. She never had a word of praise for me. As for Monsieur Lemaître, he never addressed us boarders. His long black cape, his immense red beard, and the lorgnons he used to blink at us whenever he was displeased were intimidating enough.

Once, during calligraphy class, as Madame Lemaître stood behind my chair watching my efforts over my shoulder, I forgot some curlicue on a letter. She said nothing, she just slapped me on the cheek with the back of her hand.

I jumped to my feet, threw my pen on the floor, and sent my copybook flying. Then I stormed out of the classroom, passing Madame Lemaître on my way. She did not try to stop me.

I walked across the school park, climbed over the wall, and went down the ladder into my grandparents' beloved garden. My grandfather was at work. I sat on my grandmother's low wooden bench among her flowers. Red tulips and pink roses were in bloom. My grandfather was caring well for them. Then his old cat came to rub against my legs and I wept until I ran out of tears.

After a while I returned to the boarding school, mostly because I knew that if I did not, somebody would come to get me.

At lunchtime, Monsieur Lemaître's lorgnons blinked at me once or twice, I thought. I imagined Madame Lemaître and her two daughters telling him about my "outrageous behavior." For some reason, I also imagined that he had told them to leave me alone. And maybe he did. I was not reprimanded or made to apologize.

Had I scared them?

Nelly stopped asking for peculiar favors.

One day, upon returning from a trip to the market, Rose reported that Raymonde, the daughter of the dry goods store owner, had failed to return from church to her mother's house the night before. A search party was already on its way, Rose said.

I knew Raymonde. Everybody knew Raymonde. She helped her widowed mother to run their store on Main Street, a very fine store where bolts of fabric were stacked up to the ceiling. Colorful yarns, precious laces, and embroidered collars and blouses were kept under glass. Raymonde was often in attendance in the store, always neatly dressed, her hairdo sober and orderly, her smile invariably welcoming. A little girl getting a spool of thread for her grandmother was treated as if she were a lady buying a pair of expensive embroidered sheets.

Two days later, the horrible news was all over the school—I never knew how, because the grown-ups were strangely silent that day. Raymonde's body had been found at the bottom of the well in her mother's garden.

There was an old well in every garden, dating back to the time no city water had been available. The wells were now used for watering the gardens, washing, and bathing.

On top of the wells houses with sturdy doors and padlocks had been built. I liked those tiny houses, shaped like old-fashioned beehives and covered with honeysuckle and roses.

My grandfather had permitted me, once, to look down into the well in his garden while he held me firmly. I had taken a furtive look into a deep, round masonry shaft. I had seen the dark water gleaming way down below, and I had shuddered.

Raymonde had thrown herself into a well like my grandfather's. The very thought of it was unbearable. And there was more. The grown-ups' whispers were not supposed to reach our ears, but they did. We knew it all. Raymonde had been tightly laced. She had been pregnant. Six months, maybe. And then somebody remembered having seen, one evening, Raymonde and the young priest, sitting side by side on the lowest step of the altar in the church. Indeed, six months or so before . . .

No bells would ring for Raymonde, a suicide; the church had rejected her soul. Nobody even knew where to bury her. There was no special plot for suicides in the graveyard of this orderly town where everyone was supposed to die according to the rules.

On Main Street, the dry goods store hid behind gray boards. The grown-ups managed to keep to themselves the time of day—or night—Raymonde was buried. A silence heavier than the earth that covered her body was already falling over her fate.

I mourned this girl with whom I had never exchanged more than smiles, "Thank you," "How much?" and "Good-bye." But I could not understand how she could have thrown herself into that deep, frightful shaft. I knew I could never have done it, no matter what. I could imagine throwing myself into a river, or into a pond I knew that reflected the clouds between its water lilies. I tried hard to imagine the stigma attached to her condition. I could not. I was too young, I guess. She must have laced herself until a time had come when she could not take it any longer, until anything would do that could put an end to it all.

And then, slowly, without wanting to admit it, I began to reproach her for what she had left behind: that grotesque body with a dead baby inside it. I resented the ugliness of her tortured ghost. My thoughts began to choke me. I would not share them with anybody, least of all with Nelly. But she wanted to have a talk with me, she said, one afternoon after school, as we were walking through the school park together.

Only a few steps away, above the wall, the foliage of my grandfather's apple tree was waving.

"I want to talk with my grandfather," I said suddenly, "and I am going down the ladder, right now. Go tell your mother!"

I climbed over the wall.

Nelly was probably too stunned to say anything. She only stared at me.

To be upset had made me wonderfully bold and carefree.

My grandfather was sitting at the kitchen table, reading out of this old leather-bound book I knew:

Gargantua and Pantagruel. He always picked that book whenever he was angry or displeased.

He looked at me over his reading glasses.

"Come, sit down," he said, as if he had been expecting me. "Listen."

He read from his book, in Old French, which, he had told me before, was not very different from what the old people in the countryside spoke when he was a little boy.

My grandfather must have modernized the old language for me, because I understood quite well. The episode he read related how the legendary giant Gargantua, after observing the inhabitants of the city of Paris for some time, had become so disgusted with their stupidity and turpitude that he could think of nothing more appropriate to do than to urinate on them from the top of Notre Dame's towers!

I giggled until I cried.

"Do you think we are any better or wiser than we were five hundred years ago when the story of Gargantua was written? I don't," my grandfather said.

I had no opinion. I was crying.

"I am as sad as you are," my grandfather said.

That was good to hear, even though I thought my grandfather sounded more angry than sad.

He took my hand and led me out into the garden. We sat side by side on my grandmother's bench. Keeping my hand in his, he waited patiently for me to quiet down.

And then suddenly, unable to keep it any longer, I said, "*Geranium* . . . that's what Grandmother said just before she died."

My grandfather was silent for a while.

"How lucky that she gave her last word to you," he finally said. "She loved you more than she ever loved anyone."

"You were sitting in the kitchen with my mother when she died," I said.

"I remember," my grandfather said. "We had been up most of the night. Do I remember! Your mother had just been telling me the silliest thing I have ever heard in my whole life! She had been happy to break her arm when she was little, she said, because I had broken mine just before. Happy to break her arm! Such nonsense! Your mother is still a little girl, in a way. We have to be patient with her, all of us."

Everything was quiet, peaceful, and somehow sad around us. On tall bushes close by, hazelnuts were beginning to ripen. My grandfather picked a few, opened them for me with his pocket knife as he had done years before when I had been too little to open them myself.

We did not have much to say after that, only that the hazelnuts promised to be good and abundant that year.

We walked back to the school together. We went in through the gate and inside to talk to Madame Lemaître. She was very pleased to see my grandfather, she said. Nelly apparently had not tattled.

"Yes, the evenings are long for an old man alone," I heard my grandfather say at some point.

"From now on," Madame Lemaître told me, "you'll go every evening to your grandfather and spend one whole hour with him. You can do some of your homework at his house."

My grandfather and I knew very well what kind of homework we would do together: reading the story of Gargantua and looking for hazelnuts. We both thanked Madame Lemaître.

After that, I visited my grandfather every day after school.

One late afternoon, we walked down Main Street to the railroad station to watch the late train go by as we had done when I was younger. We passed the dry goods store, which had reopened for business. This was a warm evening, the glass doors were wide open.

My grandfather took my hand, we retraced our steps and entered the store. The store owner came forward to meet us. She was dressed all in black and her face was chalk white.

My grandfather said nothing, he only took both her hands in his and looked down at her, shaking his head sadly. Then we walked out.

"*Merci, Monsieur,*" I heard the store owner whisper.

I thought the month of July, the last month of the school year, would never come to an end. The classes were relaxed. We searched fields and roadsides for rare flowers, we drew stars on the blackboard, we knitted baby jackets, and we finished reading *Les Misérables.*

Every evening after school, Monsieur Lemaître went to the forest to search for rare mushrooms, not the delicious cèpes, a specialty of the area that would pop up on the forest floor in September. (Everybody would look for cèpes then, and broil or stew them every night. Cartloads of them would be sent to Paris every day.) Monsieur Lemaître was interested only in early, rare mushrooms that nobody else ever touched.

One evening, Monsieur Lemaître came home with three of them in his basket. Small, gray, greenish, purple, with long, weak, pale stems, they definitely looked poisonous.

Monsieur Lemaître entrusted his mushrooms to Rose, ordered her to cook them in plenty of butter and serve them to him at supper.

"*Non, Monsieur*," Rose said as she took the basket. She started to cry.

At supper, right after the soup, Rose, sniffing loudly and dabbing her eyes, served to Monsieur Lemaître three brown marble-sized pellets that tossed around on a blue enamel plate.

Nelly grabbed her father's arm. "*Papa, Papa*, I want to die with you!"

Madame Lemaître shoved her plate toward her husband's.

"*Mon ami . . .* " she said firmly.

Lily, in tears, hanging onto her mother's arm, screamed that she wanted to die with her mother.

Monsieur Lemaître silently protected his shrunken mushrooms with both hands for a while. Then, grumbling that there would not be enough left for him to taste, he gave a tiny piece each to wife and daughters.

That evening, Rose had to make beds for Nelly and Lily in their parents' bedroom.

Next morning, the birds singing in the trees of the park woke us up as usual. We washed up quickly and tiptoed down the broad chateau stairs. Some of the younger boarders, I was quite sure, expected a tragedy, although none dared to utter a word about it. I, rather coldly, imagined four coffins lined up alongside the piano in the salon.

We entered the kitchen-refectory. Monsieur Lemaître was seated at the head of the table as usual, dropping chunks of butter into his chocolate milk to cool it off.

The next time the mushroom comedy was repeated at the dinner table, I suffered a fit of giggles that did little to endear me to the Lemaître family. I was ordered to go wash my face. I did not get a chance to finish my supper that evening.

At last I packed to go home for the long summer vacation, dreaming that the near future would be as the past had been—quiet, sunny, and pleasantly lonely. My grandfather would come every weekend. I would spend one or perhaps two weeks with Odette—I had so much to tell her. I would visit The Nest in the Woods. The faraway future—that is, whatever would happen after the summer vacation—was an unknown that I refused even to try to imagine.

To say good-bye to the Lemaître boarding school was easy. To say good-bye to my grandparents' lovely town was another matter. It hurt to leave, yet I wanted to leave. Something had happened to the quiet streets lined with well-trimmed linden trees, to the friendly stores, the beautiful gardens, the chateaus half hidden behind the trees of their ancient parks, even to my grandmother's flowers. Ashes had fallen over them.

My grandfather asked whether I wanted to take a walk around town with him. Yes, I wanted to. If anyone could make things look right again, it would be my grandfather.

We went through the beautiful park of the baron's chateau. My grandfather had worked there so often, he was free to come and go as though he owned it a little. We even met the baron. My grandfather lifted his worker's cap, the baron lifted his fine straw hat, and they had a friendly chat.

"Your granddaughter is turning into a pretty young lady," the baron said. "I remember how tiny and pale she was not so long ago."

"Did you hear what the baron said?" my grandfather asked afterwards.

"Yes, a lot of nonsense!"

I knew I was not pretty and would never be. My mother had told me often enough how plain I was. My forehead was too high for a girl, she had said, my mouth too big, my nose crooked, and my freckles— my freckles were a disgrace.

"My mother always told me . . . " I began.

"Oh, your mother!" my grandfather said. "Your mother is not an expert on pretty girls, but the baron is!"

I laughed, really laughed for the first time in many days.

Then we went to see the "Chinamen" who were working in the chateau's laundry. It had greatly entertained me, when I was six, to watch them filling up their mouths with water and blowing it out in a fine mist to sprinkle the white linen before ironing it. The same spectacle now disturbed me. "Grandfather, is it not odd that young Chinese men have to leave their faraway country to come do that kind of work for the rich men in our own country?"

"Odd in a way, yes," my grandfather said. "But someday these boys will have scraped together enough money to return home as proud men. And they will have seen the big world in the bargain. Not so bad, you see."

As we walked back, we passed Aunt Berthe's house. Sure enough, she saw us. She called for us to come in.

But my grandfather, even before he consulted his watch, said, "No, thank you, we can't. What do you think Madame Lami would say if we were late for supper?"

After my grandmother's death, the next-door neighbor, Madame Lami, had been preparing my grandfather's meals. For nothing in the world would he have made her wait for him.

Anyway, I knew he would never consent to sit in Aunt Berthe's house. My grandfather bore grudges. So did I.

The next morning we made several packages of my clothes and books and tied them up onto our bicycles for the trip to my parents' home. We looked forward to the ride on that gorgeous summer morning.

Before entering the forest we passed a field that had been left fallow as long as I could remember. Scattered over it were seven boulders. Smoothed out by ages of rain, frost, and snow, gray with lichen, they looked like ancient animals asleep in the grass.

"Where did those giant rocks come from?" I had asked the question before.

"Gargantua strolled by once—a long time ago, you understand—his sabots filled up with pebbles. He shook them off, right here . . . "

"Grandfather, you gave me that fancy explanation when I was six years old. I am thirteen and a half now!"

"Well," my grandfather said, "I know other explanations, but they are boring, besides being, very probably, wrong. A fancy explanation has at least two advantages over all the others, it is fun and one remembers it."

We entered the forest. The birds, exhausted by their predawn songs, were silent. Our tires made a light swish on the damp gravel of the road, and now and then crushed a dead leaf.

The narrow road was not well traveled. A strip of grass grew in the middle of it and, as always in warm weather, large, healthy slugs, a glossy orange, crisscrossed the road and grass in splendid unconcern.

We called it our road, we so rarely met anyone on the way.

And this was our enchanted forest, deep, dark, mysterious, and yet familiar because of our forays into its secret heart.

This ride together through our forest would be our last.

Immortelles

"You are little Mimi, aren't you?" said a pretty young woman who had come to a stop a few feet away from me on the cooperative's sidewalk.

She wore a stylish black and white dress and that year's fashionable hat, which completely covered the head.

"That's what everybody called me when I was little," I said. Then I recognized the green eyes, the thin lips, the mocking smile. "You are Léonie," I said.

"You finally decided to grow taller," Léonie said.

"You look different too."

"Well, I am not trying to play the country girl any longer!" Léonie laughed. "Amazing, I have not seen you once in all these years. I always come in August to tidy up Solange's grave. Today I pulled those scraggly forget-me-nots. The daisies do well, don't they?"

I was staring at Léonie. How elegant she was! Her golden hair had been cut short. Two strands shaped like question marks and pasted to her cheeks came out from under her hat. *Accroche-coeurs*, heart hooks, we called them. Only bold, smart girls wore *accroche-coeurs*.

"I have to catch my train. Why don't you come with me to the station? We can talk on the way."

We walked side by side across the bare town square.

"The village has not improved a bit," Léonie said. "Am I glad we moved back to Paris!"

I had nothing to say to that.

Suddenly Léonie put her arm around my shoulders.

"I must tell you something," she said. "It was stupid of me, stupid, but I hated you for having survived when Solange died."

"Me too," I said.

"What? What did you say?"

"Me too, I hated myself for not having died instead of Solange."

"Oh, what did you know? You were just a poor, sickly little kid! But I, I should have known better. Grief makes one dumb."

"Solange was so healthy-looking and so beautiful," I said, "and I was so plain. I was always sick anyway."

"Solange had been given too much too soon, maybe. She never had to fight for anything . . . And so, when death winked, she went along. You, I bet you fought like a little devil! That's all you knew, fighting!"

We were now standing on the platform. Our gaudy little train rolled in, clattering and smoking.

Léonie climbed into the first compartment, lowered the rattling window, and bent over.

"I am studying to become a doctor," she shouted. "I'll know someday why the beautiful are snatched away rather than the . . . "

Her last words were lost in the hooting of the locomotive.

She waved, laughing that great witch laugh that did not frighten me any longer. I waved back.

Our household was in a turmoil. Because of me. My parents could not decide to which school to send me.

Madame Lemaître had told them that, since I would never amount to much anyway, it would be a waste of money to send me to the lycée. Both her daughters would go to the lycée.

There were, in those days, two school systems: secondary school (lycée) and primary school. As far as I understood, at the lycée one studied Latin and Greek, could specialize early and terminate with the prestigious *baccalauréat* in either science or the humanities. At the primary school one studied neither Latin nor Greek, could not specialize, and ended up with the modest *brevet supérieur*. A few years later, too late for me, the *baccalauréat* and the *brevet supérieur* would be ruled equivalent.

For the sciences student, the differences in the two systems created no problem. For the humanities student, no Latin and no Greek was a stamp of inferiority that could not be erased.

Influenced by Madame Lemaître's advice—and against Monsieur Bertrand's—my parents opted for primary school, and my fate was sealed. After four years of schooling I would have the choice between becoming a post office employee or—if I could pass the difficult entrance examination to a special college—

studying three years at the government's expense, then becoming an elementary-school teacher. And perhaps, if I could get very high marks at the *brevet supérieur,* I could win entrance to the Sorbonne. A dream.

I knew that I did not want to be sitting in a cubicle selling stamps, nor did I want to teach little children. And yet these were the only two professions deemed suitable for a girl of my standing in those days. I did not even dare tell my parents—or anyone else—that I would have wanted to become a doctor. I knew how they would have laughed. I hoped, secretly, that when the time came, I would manage to avoid the snares set out for me. I had no idea how.

By the time Odette came to spend a week with me, it had finally been decided that I would go to stay at Pension Postel in Versailles and attend a high school of good repute nearby. Pension Postel, a small private school, took in boarders who attended other schools.

Versailles! I knew about the famous palace and gardens of the Sun King in Versailles. I was proud of my parents' choice.

My grandfather had misgivings. "It's too far away to come home every weekend, and that's no good," he said.

My mother was hard at work on my dresses, skirts, and coat. She had no misgivings.

Odette helped me sew tiny squares of linen with the number seven embroidered on them to every piece of clothing I would take with me. We did not mind the tedious work, we had so much to talk about.

Odette had become unhappy with life in the little house by the railroad tracks. Her mother had remarried, and her stepfather was all right, she said, but she was bored.

As a "ward of the nation," and provided she got good grades, all her studies would be paid by the government. But Odette did not want to study. She wanted to go to Paris.

"What do you want to do in Paris all by yourself?" I wondered.

She did not know. She simply had lost patience with country living.

"If Léonie could become a Parisian, so could I," she declared.

She already had a scheme.

"My cousin who lives near Paris is getting married. Of course I'll go to her wedding. Once I am there, I'll find a way to stay."

Odette was now a head taller than I. She was very pretty and, I had to admit, did not look like a schoolgirl at all. She had always been strong. She probably could take her life into her own hands. I admired her. I knew I could not be like her. I would always let grown-ups guide me, even when I did not like their choices.

One day I told Odette about my encounter with Madeleine. In a dream, I said.

"That was Solange," Odette said. "She forgave you."

"Forgave me?"

"Yes. Solange never looked as if she were going to die. You did. You had the same illness. Everybody thought you were going to die."

I hurried to tell how Léonie had explained why I had survived when Solange had not.

"Could be. Who knows?" Odette said.

But I could tell she had lost patience with the past. She wanted to talk about the future.

"You will be at Pension Postel in Versailles and I will be staying at my cousin's. We will be neighbors again. We will visit a lot. You could come spend every weekend with me. Why not?"

I did not know whether to believe in Odette's dream, but it made us happy to nurture and embellish it.

On the last day of September—my new wicker trunk having been entrusted to our local train the evening before—my father, my mother, Eliane, and I set out for Versailles. Very early in the morning we cycled to the next town. Eliane was almost too heavy for her basket on my father's bicycle. We got on the big train. It took three hours to reach Versailles. By midday a taxi deposited us, together with my trunk, in front of tall iron gates on top of which Pension Postel was written in tall black letters.

Behind us was a wide avenue lined with big trees.

"The road to Paris," my father said. "Only fourteen kilometers away."

He pulled a chain that hung by the gate, and a bell rang in the distance.

A maid unlocked the gate for us. She helped my father carry my trunk through a garden full of dahlias in bloom. We entered a building covered with vines that were turning orange and red. It all looked neat and pretty.

The maid invited us to sit in a parlor that, to my eyes, was sumptuous. Oriental rug on the floor, golden clock on the marble mantelpiece, armchairs with fragile legs and seats of pale green plush we hardly dared to sit on.

Mademoiselle Sylvie Postel, the directress, walked in. Her hair was bobbed, her skirt short, and she smiled a lot. Then Mademoiselle Hortense Postel, her older sister and the pension's manager, came to greet us. She was tall and thin. Her wide skirt came down to her ankles and her blouse had a boned, high-neck collar of black lace. Her gray hair was gathered into a bun on top of her head in yesteryear's fashion.

The two ladies shook our hands, smiled, and said that Eliane was very pretty. Nevertheless, they intimidated me. Perhaps because they were so different in spite of being sisters.

We were shown the vast refectory in the same building. It opened on a spacious square yard shaded by big old trees. On two sides there were very high walls, on the other sides, open galleries that led to study rooms. The dormitory was located on the second floor above the study rooms.

My room was a cubicle surrounded by curtains.

"That way," Mademoiselle Hortense explained, "the girls have privacy but are never alone."

My mother got busy transferring my clothes from my trunk to a small closet by my bed. My father and I went to the school I was going to attend the next day. It was a pleasant fifteen-minute walk under the trees of the avenue.

We were received by the directress, a large, smiling lady.

My father explained that I had entered school later than other children because of illness, that I had attended a very old-fashioned school for the past year, and that I probably would need some remedial classes.

"The girls are going to take an examination to-morrow. Don't worry, that will tell us in which class she belongs," the directress said.

We returned to the pension. My mother was waiting for us, pacing back and forth in the front yard.

"We are going to miss the train," she said.

We said good-bye. My father was pale. Eliane, holding onto my mother's hand, kept waving at me. The iron gates slammed shut. I began to cry.

I cried for one whole month, with and without tears, day and night.

Oddly enough, I passed the exam so well I was made to skip a class. And so there I was, together with thirty other girls, most of them older than myself, which only added to the panic that had seized me the moment my parents had left.

I could find interest in nothing. We were taken for an outing to the woods nearby. We picked up chestnuts and Mademoiselle Hortense roasted them for us. Everybody enjoyed that. I did not. Those chestnut woods had made me unbearably homesick for my forest and its infinite variety.

We were taken to the palace. I looked at the celebrated ponds, statues, and palace through a dense mist of despair; beauty, majesty, mythology, history were totally wasted on me.

I wrote a desperate letter to my grandfather. His answer came by return mail. "I am not surprised at all," he wrote. "You have a touch of that disease your great-grandfather suffered from. Only time can heal it. The Christmas vacation is only two short months away. Count the days. I am counting them too."

He had added a tiny calendar and a five-franc note to his letter.

I wrote to my parents, "I have taken an irrevocable decision. I don't want to study. I want to become a dressmaker. Mother can teach me at home. Come get me. I want to go home."

On the last Sunday of October I was called to the parlor. My parents, the directress, and the manager were there, all looking very stern. I knew what they were going to say before they said it: "No, no, no, you are not going home today!"

"Every girl who leaves her home for the first time gets disoriented for a while. It is only normal," Mademoiselle Sylvie said.

"Your daughter," Mademoiselle Hortense told my parents, "is a bit different. The other girls usually stop moping after two weeks. You will have to talk to her teachers."

We went to see the math teacher, a gray old maid who had completely bewildered me in class, she talked so fast and covered the blackboard with figures and numbers at such a speed.

At her home she was quiet, smiling, and kind. My father asked her to tutor me in math. It would surely help me, he said.

The math teacher smiled. "She does not need any tutoring, she will catch up. I know she will. She is homesick. Well, of course she is. And she should be. But, that too shall pass . . . "

"The Christmas vacation is exactly forty-seven days away," she whispered to me when we took leave.

Then we went to the literature-history-geography teacher, Madame Bailly. She lived in a lovely house surrounded by a secluded garden. She was about my mother's age, beautiful, and smartly dressed.

After listening to my parents, she spoke to me.

"Let's make a deal," she said. "If, one month from today, you still feel as you do now, we will let you go home."

She made my parents promise that they would come to get me if, after this one-month trial, I asked them to do so.

One month later, my essays were getting the highest marks, geometry and algebra had begun to make sense, and Mademoiselle Hortense smiled knowingly whenever I held my plate for a second helping of the excellent food she served us.

As for the palace's gardens, I could see now how beautiful they were. Intriguing, too. Their inhabitants, these Greek gods and goddesses, heroes and nymphs, autumn leaves falling over their marble shoulders, were exiles—like me. I would have no peace until I knew everything about every one of them.

My dear Odette,

I really hope that you have changed your mind and are now back in school. Studying is nice. I love my school in Versailles. My teachers are very good. If only you could be in my class I would be so happy. Some girls are nice but most

*are older than I am and so they don't pay much
attention to me. Would you believe it, I am the
shortest too!*

*The Pension Postel is a lot more fun than the
Lemaîtres' boarding school. We can talk and
laugh at the table and nobody scolds us.*

*We walk back and forth to school four times
a day. That's fun too. We see all kinds of people
and automobiles whizzing by. Believe it or not, I
can tell a Renault from a Citroën already.*

Write soon.

I wrote three letters to Odette before I received a
short note giving me her new address at her cousin's
home.

Odette was working in an office, she wrote. She
had told her employer that she was seventeen, and he
had believed her.

Amazing Odette, who could single-handedly real-
ize her dream!

I took the big train home for Christmas vacation
and waved at Odette's little house from the train window, even though I knew she was not there.

At home a change for the best had taken place. My
mother too had realized her dream. She loved to tell
about it.

Monsieur Bertrand's secretary, pretty Louise, and
two of her friends had one day made a surprise visit.
My mother had sewed dresses for them, of course, as
she always did, without accepting payment.

"From now on," Louise had told my mother, "you
will have to accept money for the work you do for us."

"It's a pleasure for me to make a dress," my mother had said.

"Well," Louise had answered, "we have decided that, if you don't accept payment, we won't let you sew one single stitch for us ever again."

"I can't be in business as a dressmaker, I am the teacher's wife. What would people say?"

"Nobody pays any attention to those old-fashioned, provincial notions any longer," the girls had declared.

My mother had had no choice. And so she was now doing what she liked best, sewing—which she had learned before her marriage but had been ashamed of even mentioning. Sewing was such a lowly trade compared to teaching.

Toto, stately in his winter fur, had arrived a few days before me, adding his dignified presence to the new harmony in the house. He took my enthusiastic greetings with great calm.

I had come home with good grades, which surprised my mother. My grandfather grumbled that he was not surprised at all. My father said nothing. He pored over my new schoolbooks. Monsieur Bertrand only smiled when I brought him the good news.

I could hardly stop talking about my new life and also about the miracle of electricity. In our village everybody was still struggling with kerosene lamps or with some carbide acetylene contraption that was cumbersome and ugly. The great Christmas tree at The Nest in the Woods had nearly one hundred real candles fastened to its branches. It was tedious to light them, watch them so that they would not start a fire, then extinguish them. The Christmas tree at Pension Postel had electric candles that I had seen lighted and extinguished as if by magic.

Eliane, her eyes big with wonder, listened to my stories. Soon I was inventing some just for her. I made her laugh. I made her cry. This was new and surprising. Eliane had always kept close to my mother, like a small baby. Now four, she seemed still to distrust everybody. My grandfather brought her a small present every time he came. She would slowly approach, snatch the present, and run back to my mother. We laughed, but deep down it made me unhappy, and I was sure that my father and my grandfather felt as I did.

Now that I had been away, Eliane wanted to come closer. Had she missed me? I never knew. But she cried when I left. I did not. I would never shed one tear again when leaving home.

I never quite understood what had happened to me during that long, terrible month of October. It was as if something had been removed—surgically, so to say—from my soul.

At the New Year's meal my mother had suggested that, at sixty-eight, my grandfather should think of resting instead of working as hard as he did.

"Resting?" my grandfather said, his face purple with anger and his eyes flashing. "I am going to work until the last minute of my life!"

The exchange had lasted only a short moment. I did not think that my grandfather's anger was justified, and I could tell my parents also were puzzled.

"I too want to work until my last day," my father said.

Then he changed the subject. He was scheduled to go to Versailles on the last Sunday of January, he said. Would my grandfather like to go with him?

"I don't visit my granddaughter. I expect her to visit me," my grandfather said.

It was then decided that I would come home for the last weekend of February.

Before I left, and to distract Eliane, who was already in tears, I asked Toto to promise me that he would wait for my next visit before going on his summer vacation.

His eyes not more than two green slits, Toto yawned.

"Toto has a lot of dreaming to do," I told Eliane. "Imagine, all his past and future adventures in the woods! That takes up a lot of dreaming time. What worries me is that he might forget all about me. Remind him every day to wait for me, will you?"

Eliane finally smiled.

I did too. It had just occurred to me that Toto and I had something in common. We both enjoyed the warmth of a home but knew that fate was waiting for us somewhere else. There was nothing we could do about that but be ready—and brave, if necessary.

I spent the three hours on the train doing the studying I should have done before and arrived at the pension feeling very self-sufficient.

Dear Odette,
    How did you spend the Christmas vacation?
I looked at your house from the train. I did not

*think you were there. Our old village is a sad,
dark place. There is no electricity there yet. I like
Versailles better.*

*There was one mishap. Monsieur Bertrand
gave me the choice between two necklaces. One
was a long string of red beads, the other a short
strand of white pearls. I picked the red beads.*

*Monsieur Bertrand shook his head. "You
will have to learn to distinguish between junk
and good stuff," he said.*

*I bet you would have picked the good stuff!
Write soon!*

No answer came.

On the third Sunday of January I was called to the
parlor before lunch.

"Your aunt is waiting for you," an overseer told me.

I could not think of any aunt who might visit me
unexpectedly, but I said nothing.

I did not recognize the lady who stood in the parlor. She was wrapped in a beige fur coat and wore a
beige cloche with a veil that covered the upper part of
her face.

The moment we were alone, she pushed up her
veil and laughed.

"Odette!" I should have guessed.

She was dressed like a woman and it suited her.

Poised and ladylike, she asked Mademoiselle Hortense permission to take me out for lunch, promised to
bring me back at two-thirty, and signed the guest
book.

I got into my navy blue coat and put on my ugly uniform hat.

"Guess what we call these hats? 'Chamber pots'!" I told Odette. "And do you know why they are such an ugly color? So that the 'Postel inmates' can always be spotted should they go astray."

Odette did not laugh much at my schoolgirl's jokes.

"You are not ashamed of me, are you? You look so chic."

"You are a high-school girl and I am your aunt," Odette said.

We walked on the stately avenues; we sat in a restaurant. Men looked at her. Women too. Some frowned. Odette was very beautiful, very grown up, and very happy. I was lost in admiration, and a little confused.

We did not have much time to talk. The trip from Odette's new home to Versailles had been much longer and more complicated than she expected.

"We are not neighbors," Odette said. "But never mind, next time I'll come to get you on a Saturday and we will have one night and one day together."

For some time afterwards I was so afraid somebody would discover my visitor had not been my aunt that I could not sleep.

On the following Sunday my father came. We had lunch—the two of us—in a cozy café near a back gate of the palace's gardens. I wanted to tell about Odette's visit, I really did, but my father wanted to hear about school. I chatted about a new course that enchanted me. It consisted of reading a novel, then writing an outline and a criticism of it.

"In my day," my father said, "we did not do anything like that before reaching college."

We went to the palace gardens. It had snowed just enough to give the silent groves' marble inhabitants and the bronze horses prancing over their frozen ponds a new, ghostly presence. Apollo's seven verdigris horses, snorting fog and shaking the snow off their manes, were my father's favorite. I liked the goddesses who were snow-bathing behind the winter trees. That was an eerie walk we had, and well worth getting our feet wet.

Hours passed too fast. Soon my father had to catch his train. He took me back to the pension. We said good-bye. Odette's visit had already become a little guilty secret.

At the end of February I went home as planned. My grandfather cycled through the wintry forest to spend the Sunday with us.

After lunch we sat outdoors in the pale sun while my parents were putting things away.

"Madame Lemaître sends her greetings," my grandfather said. "Nelly and Lily are terribly sorry that you did not go to the lycée with them. They are very lonely."

I said nothing.

My grandfather was keeping his hands at rest on his knees. I stared at them as if seeing the thin, brittle, reddish skin and the protruding veins for the first time.

"Why are your veins so swollen?" I asked suddenly.

"Who sees his veins, sees his pains," my grandfather quoted. He smiled. He traced the veins on my wrist with his index finger.

"My old veins are not like your young ones," he said. "Yours are small and blue. Well, blue . . . of course! There is blue blood in those veins of yours. You did not know that. I am the only one left to know the big secret. I'd better pass it on to you. My father, your great-grandfather, was the son of a baron. No, no . . . a count. Yes, a count. Oh, never mind, a blue blood in any case. Your great-great-grandfather was a blue blood."

I laughed, "He was not Gargantua, by any chance?"

"Listen, this is a true story. Your great-grandfather's mother was a poor girl. She was a maid at the local chateau. Sixteen, pretty, and unmarried . . . One day she came home to give birth to a baby, a boy, registered at City Hall as 'of unknown father.' Well, everybody in the village knew who the father was! No less than the owner of the chateau, the count of . . . Oh, darn, I have forgotten his name. My mother got the information from the two old aunts who raised the boy. Well, anyway, now you know why your veins are so blue."

I held up my hands, smiled at them.

"And now, don't go tell your mother about that!" he said. "You know your mother. Even though it all happened far from here, in the Auvergne, and a long, long time ago, she would make a big fuss. You can tell your father."

My grandfather cycled home shortly after, and I took the train to Versailles.

I received one of his cheerful short letters. As usual, a five-franc note was enclosed.

Spring's on the way.
Birds are singing.
Buds are peeking.
The woods are waiting for you and me.
*   —Your grandfather*
P.S. Twenty-six days until Easter vacation.

Before I had time to answer, I was called home by telegram for his burial. Mademoiselle Hortense put me on the next train.

"Grandfathers die," she told me. She said this several times. It did not make sense.

Hours later, I stood in my grandparents' silent house, begging my father to have the coffin opened so that I could see my grandfather one last time. During the trip home I had been thinking that if I could only see him once more, I would be all right somehow.

My father looked pained and embarrassed.

"Grandfather had a cerebral hemorrhage," he said. "You must understand, the body had to empty itself of blood . . . Trust me, you don't want to see him."

My mother was in bed in a neighbor's house. She did not want to see me or anyone else. Eliane was being shuffled from one relative to another and stuffed with candy.

I went to Madame Lami. We sat together on rickety chairs in her messy backyard.

"He came for his supper, you know, as he did every night after your grandmother died," she said. "I saw him from the window when he left his bicycle at the gate as usual. He did not look tired or anything. He was laughing . . . He came in, sat at the kitchen table, as he always did. I knew he had something to tell. He always did, you know. 'Madame Lami,' he said, 'you won't believe what I just saw. Our new baker, the one on Main Street, the smart one, you know . . . When I passed by, he was beating his automobile with a stick . . . as if it were his poor old donkey.'

"Well, I surely laughed. I was there standing in front of my stove, stirring my sauce and laughing . . . Suddenly I felt a chill. I was laughing alone . . . Your grandfather sat still, his back to the wall, his elbow on the table, his cheek resting in his hand . . . I called him, I tiptoed to him. I did not dare to touch him. He was gone, gone . . . I could not believe it! Your grandfather died laughing," Madame Lami said, and tears rolled slowly down her old cheeks.

We buried him next to my grandmother. The modest truncated column he had designed for her grave would serve for both.

The graveyard was filled with people, many of whom I did not know.

Monsieur Poret, the mayor, solemn and awkward in a black suit, stood by my grandfather's coffin and spoke calm, kind words.

Monsieur Poret was primarily our pharmacist, a gray-bearded gentleman in a snow-white coat. Once— I must have been five or six—he had come down from behind the pharmacy's high counter of polished wood to operate on my infected left hand. We had sat together in the cool, eerie light that filtered through the blue fluid of giant alchemist's bottles standing in the wide window. The air had been pungent with unknown and healing smells.

"It's not going to hurt," Monsieur Poret had said.

I had believed him. I had watched as he cut the livid skin all around the palm of my hand with small scissors rounded at the tip. It had not hurt at all.

"Brave little girl," Monsieur Poret had said then.

" . . . a brave man," he was saying now.

Then a city councillor took Monsieur Poret's place. He told how my grandfather had, many years before, lost the contract for the building of a new classroom. Less than a year later, a mighty crack had appeared in one of the new classroom's walls, and God knows what would have happened next if my grandfather had not come to the rescue. "Yes, he had consented to repair shoddy work done by someone less honest than himself . . . a generous man."

More old men in black, their faces pale and gaunt or red and bloated, eulogized my grandfather. They spoke of his goodness, his kindness, and of their everlasting respect. They went on and on, repeating the same things. Men my grandfather had disliked promised they would never forget him. I knew how this would have infuriated him. It infuriated me. My heart was beating in my throat. I wanted to scream. With my teeth clenched and my eyes tightly shut, I saw what I wanted to see: the coffin's lid lifting up and my grandfather, giantlike, standing up and shaking his shroud at them . . .

Dead silence fell. Somebody nudged me. I had to open my eyes. The coffin had been lowered into the earth. The time had come to walk to my grandfather's grave and throw my immortelle into it. I stared into the pit. Same red, ocher, wounded earth. Same coffin covered with yellow strawflowers like Solange's. Why, why do freethinkers who do not believe in immortality feel that they have to bury their dead under a blanket of immortelles? My irreverent grandfather too must have wondered about that, and smiled. Or laughed . . . laughed.

At last, it was all over. I knew what I wanted to do. Go away with my father. But that would not be permitted. Aunt Berthe had taken upon herself the duty of serving coffee, brioches, and the local eau-de-vie to the mourners at her house. And I had to help.

Nothing had prepared me for what I was to overhear. Some old people spoke too loudly.

"That's the way to go," they said. "A good death and a good life he had."

"You bet, he made it good!"

"He surely did! Remember . . . the widow Dukas?"

"I saw his bicycle parked in her backyard often enough."

"Did she come?"

"I did not see her, did you?"

"Oh, she must be getting old, too."

I aimed at the gossips what I wished could be my grandfather's icy blue glare. They did not even notice. I went to sit in a corner of Aunt Berthe's vast dining room with Madame Lami.

"He always took such good care of your poor sickly grandmother," she said. "Once, I recall, she complained about her wheelbarrow being too heavy. The next day, your grandfather started to work with the carpenter. He had no peace until he had come up with the neat, light wheelbarrow that your grandmother loved. She complained about the city laundry being too crowded. Your grandfather rented that nice meadow down the road. There is a warm spring there, and that's a luxury around here, you know. From then on, your grandmother had the best private laundry in the whole town."

I knew about the wheelbarrow. And I knew about the laundry. In winter, steam hovered over the spring and over the rivulet that brought water into two cemented pools. Grandfather had mended the shed built over the pools. This was truly a very special laundry.

"Did the widow Dukas come to my grandfather's burial?" I asked.

Madame Lami turned towards me. We stared at each other.

Tiny, incongruous gold earrings shone in her elongated, wrinkled earlobes. A hat made of shiny black stuff sat on top of her white hair, absurd and dignified. There was only kindness in her old gray eyes.

She took my hand and held it in her strong, rough hands. Her voice low and tired, she said: "He was a man."

Something I was not yet ready to understand.

I went back to school with anger in my heart. Pompous eulogies and nasty gossip seemed to be all I could remember. I was also angry with my mother.

She had refused to see me during the two days I had spent at home after the burial.

Two weeks later when I returned for Easter vacation, she was still in bed and still refused to see anyone. She had declared, my exhausted father told me, that since she had not one single reason to go on living, she was going to die. She would not even take notice when Eliane slipped into her bedroom and crouched at the foot of her bed.

If Louise had not come to the rescue, I don't know what we would have done. Orphaned when a baby, raised by poor relatives, she had, by chance, found shelter at The Nest in the Woods. Before the age of eighteen, she had already become Monsieur Bertrand's secretary. She was resourceful.

Louise came to visit my mother.

"She won't see anybody," we told her.

Louise smiled. She calmly climbed the stairs, knocked on my mother's bedroom door, and went in without waiting for an answer. We heard her turning the key in the lock.

Over an hour later, she came down, assured us that everything would be fine, and left.

The next day my mother got up. Soon, she had resumed a normal life. She did not speak much and she was very sad. But then, so were we.

At the end of my vacation I paid a short visit to The Nest in the Woods.

"Louise, what did you do to cure my mother?" I asked.

"I told her I had overheard your father tell Monsieur Bertrand that if his wife could not get hold of herself, he would just have to leave. He did not have the stamina to cope with that kind of situation."

"Did my father really say that?"

"Well, not quite," Louise laughed. "But Monsieur Bertrand had said that we had to do something to help you people."

Geranium

One month or so before the end of the school year I got, for the first time, a low grade on an essay written in class. The subject had been something about maternal love. I had spent precious time fidgeting. Then, at the last minute, I had dashed off a story about a mother cat.

Madame Bailly called me at recess time.

"A mother cat is all right," she said. "But, tell me, couldn't you write something about the love of your own mother?"

"My mother was always sick when I was little. She kept searching for a doctor who could cure her. Maybe she did not have time . . . "

I stopped. I was not in the habit of talking so much to a teacher.

"I see," Madame Bailly said. She put her arm around my shoulders.

"My mother recovered her health after my sister was born," I said. "It's why she loves my sister so much, I guess."

Madame Bailly smiled.

"Maybe so," she said, "but remember, you have a father who loves you enough for both a father and a mother. You are not missing anything."

This was, in a way I did not try to understand, a very comforting talk. Afterwards, Madame Bailly and I often exchanged little smiles. I was almost sorry to go home for the summer vacation—the first without Odette and without my grandfather.

Before I had time to unpack, my mother once more surprised us.

"We can afford two weeks at the seashore," she announced.

She had already picked out a fishing village in southern Brittany.

We had been at the seashore the last time during the summer that had preceded the war. Nine years had passed since then. I had vague memories of gray skies, gray waves, and gray round stones that rolled under my feet. I also had an older memory—me, age two or three, wading into lapping, warm waves with my arms outstretched, intent on catching an enormous red sun before it vanished into a dark ocean. A man had fished me out and handed me dripping wet to my screaming mother. After so many years, she would still blush in anger whenever the incident was mentioned, and I could still smile at the magic of that lost moment.

My mother and I spent two frantic weeks fixing clothes and packing them into a trunk, my father found substitutes for his different jobs, and we were on our way. After one whole night on the train we arrived at a quiet fishing village. Its low houses all faced a bay where boats and seabirds floated. Its one hotel, where we stayed, built of dark stone like the village houses, had only one story and was very plain. But in its yard grew plants I knew from pictures only—a palm tree that almost reached up to the roof and oleanders in full bloom.

"The Gulf Stream," my father said. "Without the Gulf Stream, Brittany and the whole of France would be like Siberia."

We both became very enthusiastic about the Gulf Stream and the miracles it made possible. And that included a long-dead civilization that had left scattered over the whole landscape strange monuments with odd names—menhir, dolmen—and no good explanation.

The sun shone every day and the waves were tame in the bay. A retired teacher my father befriended taught me to swim. Eliane refused to go near a water that moved back and forth and contained little crabs, which she called spiders. At the end of the first week she consented to wade up to her ankles, provided she wore a jacket over her swimsuit. My father built sand castles for her. She had tantrums when the tide washed them away.

"At least we have one daughter who will never try to catch the setting sun," my mother said.

One day, together with another family, we went across the bay in a sturdy fishing boat. Strong fishermen manned the oars. We all felt very good. Then, as we were reaching the middle of the bay, without warning the sky turned dark and the waves swelled up. Our boat seemed to turn into a toy, tossing up and down as it did. We all got scared, held onto the railings or crouched at the bottom of the boat. All except my mother. She sat upright, swaying with the boat, smiling and saying "Oops" as if it had all been a game. Her performance kept Eliane from getting too frightened.

When we reached port, the fishermen, who usually spoke little, complimented my father for having such a brave wife.

We returned home. I described our two memorable weeks in a long letter to Madame Bailly. "And from now on it will be just knitting and sewing," I wrote in conclusion. I received a prompt answer. "Take long walks, alone if you have to, ride your bicycle, don't sit and dream too much," Madame Bailly wrote.

The next morning I got up with the sun and took a long walk in the woods that surrounded the castle. These were lovely woods, not as dark as the old forest, but big enough. It took over one hour to cross them in any direction. And Toto was there. I called him. I imagined him climbing down a tree and coming to rub his back against my legs. I would not try to grab him, I promised. He did not show up. I had not really thought he would. He probably turned into a wild cat the minute he returned to the wilderness and forgot all about us until he got cold. A bit sad, but, who knows, as it should be, perhaps.

I took a long walk every day at sunrise.

"This is not normal behavior for a young girl," my mother said.

She took me to an old doctor who had a practice in a neighboring town. The doctor listened to my mother and smiled.

"Normal or not, this is very healthy behavior for a young girl," he said. He sent us on our way without accepting payment for his services. This infuriated my mother.

I cycled with Monsieur Bertrand's secretary Louise through the countryside, which was something my mother did approve of. She made us one white pleated skirt each.

Once as we were riding through a small village, Louise's front bicycle wheel went into dry sand on the gravel roadside and she was thrown to the ground. She picked herself up without a word of complaint. Her arm and leg were bleeding. She pointed at tiny pebbles and dark specks embedded in the wounds.

"That won't do," she said. "Too much horse manure around here."

She knocked on the door of the nearest farm-house, asked for water, soap, chlorine water, and a good strong brush.

I watched her scrubbing her bloody arm and leg as if they were laundry. She got out all traces of dirt. I got sick in my stomach.

"I don't want to get tetanus," she said to the farmers who were watching the proceedings, shaking their heads and mumbling.

"And you, you'll know what to do in case you need to," she told me.

I nodded and shuddered.

I wrote several long letters to Odette during that summer and received one short answer before returning to school. Odette would come to get me on a Saturday, she wrote. "Ask your father for a written authorization to spend a whole weekend with your aunt," she added.

When I returned to school my father cycled with me to the railroad station.

"Write only about good grades, good people, good weather, good everything . . . You know your mother," my father said.

He promised he would come to visit me on the last Sunday of October.

In Chartres, the train stopped for twenty minutes. As usual, I looked out. For once, there was someone I knew—Cousin Hélène, Aunt Berthe's youngest daughter, and her husband. There was room in my compartment, and they joined me. Hélène's wedding had taken place two weeks before. My parents and I, still in mourning, had not attended. I was meeting Hélène's husband for the first time. He had red hair and a red mustache. I did not like him; he reminded me of the red-haired doctor.

I had always admired Cousin Hélène. She had the skin of a china doll—pink, white, and flawless—and the hair of an angel—pale gold and the right amount of natural curls.

"We are going to spend one week in Paris," Hélène said. "Then we will buy a store like my mother's but in a bigger town. My husband quit his teaching position to marry me." She was quite proud of that.

After a while, it got stuffy in the compartment. We could not open a window because Hélène feared drafts, so I went into the hall to get some fresh air. Hélène's husband joined me. He asked about my school and my grades. I chatted a bit giddily about pension and school. He laughed. He regretted that I had not attended the wedding, he said, and was so glad to have met me at last.

"You are turning into quite a young lady," he said.

This irritated me, since he had never seen me before.

"We are cousins now," he said. "I think it's wonderful, don't you?"

"Well, I don't know," I said. "Your wife is my father's cousin, not mine, really. I don't think that marrying my father's cousin makes you my cousin . . . "

He laughed.

"Yes, yes, I am your cousin," he said. "And that gives me the right to kiss you when we part."

I felt my face burning as I went back to my seat. I had not wanted to talk so much to Hélène's husband. I was angry at myself. I tried to resume my conversation with Hélène. I could not find much to say. Anyway, she dozed off. The train ride lasted forever.

At last we reached Versailles. I kissed Hélène good-bye and hurried out. Her husband took my suitcases down from the luggage rack and handed them to me through the window. And right away he was beside me on the platform. I knew he was going to kiss me. I offered my cheek. But he grabbed my head with both hands and kissed me, not as a decent cousin would, on both cheeks, but on the mouth as lovers do. I shoved him away with all my strength, got hold of my suitcases, and ran, bumping into people. Hélène's image danced before my eyes. Cute, contented Hélène. I aimed at her my rage, my shame, my hatred all balled into one, as though it had been she who had inflicted upon me the insult of such a lover's kiss—my first.

The incident tormented me a good deal during the following weeks. And it was not easy to think about it clearly. To begin with, it was not poor Hélène who deserved my hatred, it was her husband. And the redhaired doctor. And most men, probably. Keep away from them, I admonished myself, keep away. Madame Bailly, Mademoiselle Sybil, Mademoiselle Hortense, and the sad women who were our overseers were the ones I would trust and love. In the past I had often resented their presence. No more. I wanted them all close to me now. The trouble was that I could not forget how much I had enjoyed the attention Hélène's husband had given me. I had enjoyed it a lot. I remembered how I had chatted and joked about pension, school, teachers, overseers, and boasted about my grades. I had loved it when he had laughed at the funny things I had said. And when he had told me that he had the right to kiss me—I could not, no matter how hard I tried, smother the memory—I had wished he would. Oh, only for a few seconds. But I had. I knew I had. And knowing it was like having a chunk of hot coal smoldering inside me. Nobody would ever know, of course. Nobody. But that did not help me much.

These were confused days. Whenever I thought of my father I wanted to cry.

He came as promised, on the last Sunday of October, a fine autumn day, sunny and quiet. We went to the palace gardens as usual.

We passed the statuary representing Laocoön and his sons fighting the deadly embrace of the serpents.

On this very spot I had, not so long ago, philosophized about cruel, unjust destiny that the ancient Greeks chose to call gods.

"Showing off their beautiful muscles," I sneered now.

My father only remarked that this particular eighteenth-century copy of a Roman copy of a Greek original happened to be conspicuous by the poor treatment of the muscles on the three men.

I said nothing for a while.

We sat on a bench in the King's Garden. No statue there, only splendid tapestries of asters and dahlias. I had a vision of King Louis the Fourteenth in powdered great wig, lace jabot, velvet breeches, and high heels, strutting among beaming ladies.

"The self-proclaimed Sun King, that egomaniac! Women were his toys," I said. "Did you know that he took them for endless rides in his carriage and would not permit them to go to the toilet?"

My father nodded. He knew.

We walked out of the gardens.

"And, of course, he ignored the cartloads of dead workers that were driven out every day when his palace and gardens were built."

My father took me to a pastry shop.

"I saw Cousin Hélène and her husband on the train when I returned to school," I said.

"I have wondered about Hélène's husband," my father said. "Never met him. All I know is that he quit his teaching position just before the wedding."

"Hélène said they were going to buy a business in a big city."

"Hélène got a nice dowry," my father said.

"Am I glad I won't get a dowry!" I said.

"You'll get a dowry," my father said, "a very, very small one."

I delayed starting on the luscious chocolate-coffee eclair—my favorite—on my plate.

"I shall spend every penny of it beforehand, I swear. And anyway, I'll never marry."

My father said nothing. I saw lines on his forehead I had not seen before. I did not want him to ever know what had happened.

Winter had arrived when Odette finally came, one Saturday afternoon. She wore a short red coat and a red hat. Nobody recognized her.

Mademoiselle Sybil had received an authorization from my father for me to spend the weekend with my friend Odette at her cousin's home.

"It would be more fun if I could still be your aunt," Odette said.

I was more comfortable with the truth.

We took a train that rolled briefly through meadows and woods and then entered what seemed to be an endless drab city. There were rows of houses and here and there large buildings with blind walls and high chimneys belching smoke. I was surprised.

"The suburbs," Odette said. "I'll show you the wealthy suburbs . . . someday."

She took off her hat and shook her beautiful ash-blond bobbed hair. Women did not take off their hats on the train or on the street in those days. I did not.

Odette laughed the way she had when she was seven.

"Watch," she said. Her eyes were full of mischief.

The train was slowing down. It came to a stop. Odette rolled down the window and stuck her head out. Men standing on the platform shouted and clapped.

She repeated the performance several times during the trip. A lady who sat in our compartment frowned. I laughed, but I did not quite know what to think.

We changed trains—this was a long trip—and finally got out at a drab railroad station. We still had to take a bus and walk a while before reaching the house where Odette's cousin lived—a small gray house, among other small gray houses, without a tree or a shrub near it.

Odette's cousin and her husband were already having supper in the kitchen when we arrived. We joined them. They did not pay much attention to me. They sat close to each other and kept kissing during the meal. I found this repulsive.

"They are such lovebirds," Odette said fondly.

After supper, Odette and I sat on her bed. Her bedroom was very small. There were pictures of actors I did not know pinned on the walls.

I could not wait to tell Odette about the awful behavior of my cousin's husband. Odette listened. She did not seem as outraged as she should have been.

"Odette," I begged, "a man two weeks married to my very pretty cousin!"

Then, I don't know why—I should have known better—I told about the red-haired doctor and his stupid promise to marry me when I was too young to understand he was joking. And how . . . well, I had never known what had happened between him and my mother.

"Beware of red-haired men," Odette said. And she laughed. I felt suddenly very lonely, seated close to my only friend. And cheated, somehow.

Then it was Odette's turn. She was telling me about her boyfriend. I did not want to listen.

"He works at the same factory as my cousin's husband. He is very nice but he is poor. And he is too young to marry. Oh, well, so am I."

"I'll never marry," I said. "I hate men."

Odette put her arm around my waist and patted my hair.

"Wait, you are still in school," she said.

"Oh, well, I love my father, and I loved my grandfather, and I like Monsieur Bertrand a lot," I said, and I finally laughed a little too.

I shared Odette's narrow bed, and I woke early next morning thinking of Pension Postel. It seemed very far away, and yet I would be there in only a few hours. I did not mind.

After breakfast, Odette decided to turn me into a Parisian. She smeared my face with cream, powdered it, applied rouge to my cheeks and lips. I did not take makeup well—one of my cheeks was redder than the other, my mouth looked crooked, and the eye shadow made me cry.

We were standing in front of a mirror. I grimaced at my new face and looked up at Odette's.

"I have never seen anyone more beautiful than you," I said.

"Yes, yes, I know," Odette said. "Everybody says I should become a cocotte."

I knew what a cocotte was. I don't know how. From grown-ups' books, probably.

"Everybody?"

"Oh, I don't know, I don't know," Odette said. "I think I love my boyfriend too much."

I did not know what to say. I was totally lost in Odette's world.

We were forbidden to play together when we were seven. Odette had a bad influence on me, the grown-ups said. I remembered that I imitated her pranks then. No danger of that now. I would certainly not follow in Odette's steps. She was beautiful. She probably had to obey her beautiful-woman's destiny. Whatever that was. Something to do with men, I imagined. I was glad I was what I was.

Odette plunked one of her hats on my head.

"Let's go to the movies," she said.

Walking beside her on the street, I felt invisible and it suited me.

The movie was about some romance I found stupid and embarrassing. Odette loved it. She knew the actors' names and even details about their private lives.

We returned to the house. I scrubbed my face at the kitchen sink and retrieved my uniform hat without displeasure.

As we were about to leave, Odette pointed at a wooden box on her dresser.

"Open it," she said.

The box contained letters. Mine. Only mine.

"You keep my letters!" Some, I remembered, were just scribbles in pencil.

"Every one of them! You write a lot, you'll surely become a writer." Odette laughed.

"My cousin says your letters might be worth money someday," Odette explained.

Now I was hurt. I said nothing, knowing I would not be understood.

Odette took me back to Pension Postel. She did not mind the tedious long trip she had to take twice that Sunday night.

"I'll come to get you another time soon," she said.

I don't know why, but I did not think she would.

Madame Bailly was the most popular of our teachers. We all waited for her arrival every morning to see what she was going to wear that day. She always wore the most becoming clothes. Smiling, she would join a group of teachers in the yard. Her smile was enchanting. She would take off her hat. Her hair was prematurely gray, which matched her gray eyes beautifully. One of us would always be waiting to take the hat and carry it to our classroom as though it were some precious object. I was timid. I did not get a chance to carry the hat often. But I could get good grades. A line of praise from Madame Bailly's blue pen on my copy was enough to fill me with the most intense joy. A slight reprimand or a frown from her could ruin my day.

On my way home for Christmas vacation, I looked at Odette's house from the train window and felt sad. I made myself write to my old friend as soon as I reached home. I could hardly find anything to say.

My mother was making a new coat for Louise, a shiny, black wraparound affair that barely skimmed the knees and was topped by an oversized collar of pale, fluffy fur.

My mother and Louise spent hours discussing fashion trends, leafing through magazines, and draping pieces of fabric over one another's hips and shoulders. They could not get me interested even in the making of my own clothes. It mattered little to me whether sleeves were puffed up or flat that year, collars nonexistent or overwhelming, skirts long or short. It mattered very much to my mother and to Louise. They said I did not have very good taste.

That year, I helped decorate The Nest in the Woods' Christmas tree. We had hardly started when Louise confided she had a fiancé. She would not stop talking about him. She wore his photograph in a medallion that hung from a chain around her neck. I found this utterly ridiculous. And besides, her young man did not look that good! Monsieur Bertrand, Louise said, was opposed to her marriage.

"I don't trust men," I said.

I was not going to explain why. I was through with confidences. Louise was not interested anyway.

I was disappointed in Louise, whom I had admired so much in the past. How could such a strong, bright girl have become so besotted all of a sudden? Nothing of that sort would ever happen to me. That much I knew.

My father was very busy. I saw him only during meals, at which time Eliane was the center of attention. She was such a good eater. Not the picky eater I had been, my mother said. That was certainly why she had such pretty pink cheeks. And no freckles, probably. I still had freckles. Many. Eliane insisted in calling them pimples, which made everybody laugh.

Our meals were hurried because of my mother's sewing. I offered to help in the kitchen. My mother refused. Whenever I set foot in the kitchen, she said, either the sauce curdled or the oil caught fire in the pan.

"The truth is," my father told me, "your mother is not a very good cook."

"Why does she blame it on me?"

"Don't pay attention. You know your mother," my father laughed.

I stayed in my room more than usual during this vacation. I built a fire in the fireplace and wrote to Madame Bailly. Toto kept me company. He had a scar across his nose and one of his ears was torn, but his purr was as loud as ever. He had arrived in October that year, which meant, according to my mother, that the winter would be long and cold. I secretly hoped this meant that Toto was getting tired of the wilderness.

I missed my grandfather. I wanted to talk about him but could not for fear of upsetting my mother.

One afternoon she was working on a dress of crimson velvet trimmed with white fur.

"It's for a girl your age," my mother said. "She has dark eyes and long black hair. She will be so pretty in that dress."

The happy colors and the evocation of a lovely picture must have put my mother into a good mood. She asked me to help her. She made me sit close to her and I pinned strips of white fur to the collar and sleeves of the dress.

Eliane was busy with her dolls.

"The red velvet reminds me of grandmother's geraniums," I said.

My mother said nothing. She went on sewing.

"*Geranium* . . . " I said. "That was her last word."

Tears slowly rolled down my mother's cheeks.

I was very small when I saw her tears for the first time. She had held me in her arms then, urging me to give a lump of sugar to her tiny brown dog. The dog sat on a high dresser, partly wrapped in a white towel. He did not take the sugar. He whimpered and had some sort of seizure. Tears swelled out of my mother's staring green eyes, slid down her soft, warm, luscious skin. The wonderment that had filled me then was still with me.

I dried my mother's tears so that they would not fall on the costly fabric and stain it. She went on sewing, did not stop before nightfall. I peeled the vegetables for the evening soup that day.

I returned to Pension Postel. We had a new overseer. Tall, skinny, and as stiff as a rod, she wore an unruly mop of yellow hair on top of her head. I named her O'Cedar. Everybody loved it. I wrote a vivid description of O'Cedar in a letter to Odette. I was about to mail the letter when I remembered the wooden box on Odette's dresser. Besides, Odette had never showed much interest in my schoolgirl stories. I shoved the letter into my desk.

Only two weeks later I received an urgent message from my father. Odette's mother had written to him that Odette was at Saint Louis Hospital in Paris and that I should visit her. The authorization to do so on the coming Sunday accompanied the letter.

Mademoiselle Sybil's written instructions in hand, I took the train for Paris, then the subway, by myself, for the first time. I reached the big, gloomy hospital at visiting time and I found Odette tucked into a cot in a long hall. There had not been room for one more bed in the crowded ward. This struck me as a bad omen.

Odette's cot was low and narrow. I kneeled on the floor beside her. She was lying on her back and smiling as brightly as ever.

"No, it's not my skin," she said. (Skin diseases were the speciality of Saint Louis Hospital.) "It's my legs! It started with my feet. One day I was riding my boyfriend's bicycle and my feet could not find the pedals. Then my legs got all silly, too. I can't walk anymore."

I did not know what to say. Was Odette's speech slurred a little? I was not sure.

"My cousin's doctor did not know what to do. But the hospital's doctors will know for sure."

I, too, trusted that the hospital's doctors would know what to do.

"I don't know what's happening to my eyes," Odette said. "I can't see you well. I'll have to wear glasses, I guess. Oh, I don't mind."

"I would not mind either," I said, which was not true.

"When you wear glasses," Odette said, "you look smart." She laughed.

I had brought her a bunch of violets. There was no vase and no side table by Odette's cot. When I slipped the violets into her cold hands, she smiled her old mischievous smile.

"We will go dancing at the Moulin Rouge when I get well," she said.

"Yes, yes, we will," I said, although I knew already that we would not.

Mademoiselle Sybil and Mademoiselle Hortense wanted to know about my friend's illness. I related what I knew, in great detail, hoping this would help them identify the disease.

All they said was that I would not be permitted to visit Odette again; this unknown illness might very well be contagious. I turned to Madame Bailly. She was just as negative. Neither Odette's mother nor her cousin answered my inquiring letters. The past was returning like a bad dream, as though the grown-ups once more were in league against my friendship with Odette. The guilt born with Solange's death and buried deep like a poisonous seed wormed itself up, grew, and blossomed anew.

My father came to spend a Sunday with me. I badgered him until he consented to leave by an earlier train, stop on his way at Odette's house, and talk to her mother.

His next letter shed no light on Odette's illness. She would soon leave the hospital to return home, he wrote. I could visit her there during the approaching vacation.

I resumed my letter writing to Odette. I wrote her every day. I chatted about everything. I had to entertain her, I thought. I had to distract her from whatever pain she might feel. I had to save her.

17 March 1923

Dear Odette,

Would you believe it, the violets are in bloom already! I saw some at the entrance of the chestnut woods last Thursday when we were on our outing. But O'Cedar would not let us pick them. "Let them be," she said, "they will only wilt in your hands." Poor, dear, old O'Cedar! I wanted to dry those violets between the pages of a book and enclose them in a letter to you.

We went picking violets together when we were little, do you remember? You always got a bigger bunch than I did.

Ten more days to go before Easter!
I'll come to visit you then.

—Your friend

On my first vacation day, I rushed to Odette.

When I arrived, her mother and stepfather had just gotten her out of bed for the noonday meal. They sat her in a high chair. She had lost so much weight that she fitted in it. They shoved her dangling legs under the seat, arranged her hands in her lap, propped her head with pillows. I held her cold hands in mine. I kissed her cheeks. She looked like a great, beautiful, broken doll. She spoke, but I could not understand her. Her mother could. "Odette says you must come for a whole week during the summer," she said. I promised I would. I spooned mashed potatoes into her mouth, very slowly. She swallowed with difficulty. I chatted. She listened. I knew she did. And she smiled too, but not much. The light had gone out of her big blue eyes, and all the mischief.

Odette's stepfather told jokes. Her mother bustled about as if unconcerned. There were new lines on her handsome face.

After the meal we carried Odette back to her bed. Her mother and I stayed with her. A train roared by, shaking the house. Odette smiled, closed her eyes, and went to sleep.

"Yes," her mother said, "yes, she loves those noisy trains."

When I left, a late afternoon fog was already wrapping the house, the trees, and the telephone poles into a gray shroud. I welcomed it with all my heart.

Odette's mother followed me out. Tears were streaming down her face. We took a few steps together. She hugged me, then gently pushed me away.

"Don't miss your train," she sobbed.

I sleepwalked towards a railroad station I could not see, Odette's mutilated image secured in the secret scrapbook that shall fall to dust when I do.

Then came the day when the mailman delivered the dreaded card—white with a black border and a cross at the center—that told us of Odette's death and the day and time of her funeral.

"You are not going!" both my parents said.

They gave no reason. I begged and I argued. Then I gave up. I understood without wanting to that they wanted to protect me from something I did not want to be protected from.

My father went. I watched him climb on his bicycle from my window. It was raining. He was the one who should not have gone, his lungs were so bad.

A day as long as a last day passed. I stared into the fire with an old cat and packed for a road unknown my untidy bundle of sorrows and grudges.

The old cat I would watch, a day or so later, limping across the meadow. Childhood's last mirage trembled at the edge of the greening woods. I did not call him back.

And then the spring sun shone over the meadow where Médor had listened to my woes, where Solange's blond ghost had walked and the echoes still played with Odette's laughter.

That too hurt. And yet, that was the way it was, as Odette would have said. The way it ought to be, perhaps. A day would come when I would put childhood's ghosts to rest, gilded and laid down flat like the images of saints in ancient manuscripts, like the words yellow with age and more precious than gold couched in the forefathers' leather-bound book. Losses turned to riches through the singular alchemy that we choose to call memory.

Epilogue

A young friend who visits often asked me one day to explain what my book is about.

"It's about the child I was," I said, "about ghosts . . . and about things that last."

My young friend was silent for some time, then she said, "Do you remember when you were writing about the grandmother who gave you her last word . . . that old geranium by the window finally bloomed, and out of season, too."

"Yes," I said. "Yes I remember."

I was fourteen when I lost the grandfather who had thrown open vast windows on the world, had taught me to hear all voices and become a slave to none, and would trample into the dust the once and future red-haired intruders. A voice inside me whispered that my grandfather would live as long as I would, and I could bear the unbearable loss.

The lesser-known grandmother, who grew only immortelles in her garden, died when I was old enough to be a grandmother myself. And I have known ever since that she would be the smiling, inexorable, ultimate guide.

She followed the path our common ancestors had traced. Doggedly and well.

"The apple trees were in bloom for your grandmother's funeral, but the church was much too small," my father wrote.

He nearly caught his death, standing in a cold spring wind by the graveyard gates to receive the condolences of the children and grandchildren of his mother's contemporaries, they came in such numbers.

I could have followed a path parallel to the one my grandmother followed. With only a little bit of her doggedness, I could have finished my studies at the Sorbonne, survived the war and the German occupation quietly, obscurely teaching. And writing, since this was all I had ever wanted to do.

But there was a wanderer among my ancestors. I taught for a short while and then one day I took a vacation in a sunny country and neglected to return. I had found work in the movies. One year passed. I eventually became homesick, went home and back to teaching. I wrote poetry, dreaming of other escapes. I married another wanderer. He and I were going to walk around the world. Yes, walk. The Second World War stopped us at the wrong hour and at the wrong place. We survived, by accident, as an empire crumbled around us. Ten years of our lives frittered away.

By the time we reached peace and the New World, our youth had gone. The New World, nevertheless, extended a warm welcome. At Columbia University, where I took English for Foreigners, my teachers offered to help with whatever I would write.

"You'll never make it," my husband said.

"You'll never make it," timorous voices inside me echoed.

I had been a teacher, a weaver, a translator, a farmer. I would be a dressmaker too. I was a dressmaker for some years in New York.

I revolted once, wrote a story for children, and for the next five years I was a children's book writer.

Then, thinking I had done my apprenticeship, I began to write for adult readers.

"You'll never make it," my husband said.

This amazingly talented man, a dancer, a musician, a painter, an illustrator and writer, who had also built factories, watched with a cold eye as I, in a fit of rage, threw an armful of manuscripts into the fire.

If I had been as strong as my grandmother . . . Well, I was not. And there is no time left for bitterness.

There was never time for boredom either.

Paris, Rome, Berlin, New York . . . I loved these big cities. But I also lived at the bottom of the gorge in a haunted house, on the top of a mountain—there was no road to get there—and in an Indian village that cast a magic spell upon me. This has been a long voyage.

I have probably reached the last station. On my front lawn, a wreath of white narcissus blooms the whole winter long. This is a good place for a last conversation with loyal ghosts.

M.M.
New Mexico
March 1996